BÊTE NOIRE
FEAR IS JUST A POINT OF VIEW

Editors:

A. W. Gifford
Jennifer L. Gifford

P. O. Box 1545
Highland, MI 48357

www.betenoiremagazine.com

Bête Noire is published by Dark Opus Press a division of Charm Noir Omnimedia P.O Box 1545, Highland, MI 48357

ISBN: 978-0615930398

"Blind Man's Bluff" first appeared on Cast Macabre, CM22

"Gothic Window" first appeaed in Aoife's Kiss, issue 23, December 2007

In This Issue

Clutterbug - Adam Howe — 1

The Masque of Medico - Florence Grey — 5

Bird N Skull - L.A. Spooner — 6

A Theory of Unremarkable Madness - J.J. Steinfeld — 8

Countess Bathoroy's Procurer - Marge Simon — 19

A-Haunting We Will Go - Fred L. Taulbee, Jr. — 21

Blind Mans Bluff - Brian G. Ross — 29

Noir People - Bruce Boston — 35

The Equilibrium of Luck - Teresa Hawk — 37

Cthulhu's Campaign Song - Robert Laughlin — 47

Gothic Window - Richard H. Fay — 49

The Flute of the Dead - Jack Campbell, Jr. — 51

Skinjacking - Sarina Dorie — 59

Love's Cadaver - WC Roberts — 61

Seeing Red - Michelle Ann King — 63

Playing Games with Death - John Grey — 67

Wicked Hybrid - R.J. Smuin — 69

The Secret of Love is Perfect Timing - H.L Fullerton — 70

Writing as a Near Death Experience - J. J. Steinfeld — 73

My Big Problem with Zombies - Phil Beloin, Jr. — 75

CLUTTERBUG

Adam Howe

Mrs. Fogle lived alone. No dog, no visitors. A stickler for routine.

Vern was huddled on the bench opposite her house, waiting for the woman to leave as she always did this time of day. His reedy legs jogging anxiously, clawing at a bony forearm that was pocked with needle—tracks; already clucking for a fix.

Right on cue, the old spinster stepped outdoors, waddling away down the street to the bus stop, pausing only to fetch a discarded Coke can from the footpath, which she crunched in her hand, delighting at the noise it made, popping it in her bag like a lipstick. *Crazy old bat.* Vern watched as she got on the bus and it puttered away.

He sloped to his feet. Ducked down the alley alongside the house. Gave a quick glance about. Seeing no—one, he slipped over the fence into the garden.

Cupping his hands to the kitchen window, Vern peered inside. Satisfied that the place was empty, he cushioned his arm with his jacket and then drove his elbow through the pane. Hardly made a sound; he was getting better at this. He wormed through the jagged hole, flopping onto the kitchen floor, rising quickly to a ninja-like crouch. Listening intently. Ready to flee at the slightest sound.

Then he saw—and smelled—the kitchen.

The counters were cluttered with dirty dishes that reeked of rotten food and mould. The sink was filled with grey-green sludge in which more crockery was frozen like pineapple chunks in jelly. The refrigerator door was covered in a rash of magnets. Stacked on top of the unit were shoeboxes filled with all sorts of odds and sods; more fridge-magnets, and milk bottle tops, and ancient food coupons, and cereal box toys. In a corner of the room was a wheelie-bin crammed with soft drink cans like the can of Coke that Vern had watched Mrs. Fogle collect; he recalled the woman's delighted grin as she'd stuffed the can in her handbag. Heaped around the bin like rocks around a lighthouse, bin bags ballooned with festering fast food cartons. Fat black flies swarmed above the bin bags, hardly able to believe their luck.

That the place was a shithole—in stark contrast to what Vern had expected from how it looked outside—didn't immediately concern him. His own flat was no great shakes. And he was here to rob the joint, not write a report for *Ideal Home*. He crept across the kitchen to the hall, the bottoms of his trainers smacking on the linoleum like toffee. The hall was lined with mouldering clothes that smelled of mothballs and old lady, a trench-like passage that wend through the clothes to the living room.

It was a junkyard. Boxes and crates filled with jumble, stacked floor to ceiling. More piles of clothes, rotted to rags. Rickety pillars of yellow newspapers, magazines and books. Mountains of broken furniture. A pram heaped with mannequin parts like the aftermath of a bomb blast. A claw-foot bathtub filled with rusted machine parts like a melted robot. A pile of worn-out mattresses sprouting springs like weeds. The ceiling was mottled with psychedelic fungus from the fetid miasma that wafted above the trash.

Vern wandered through the maze of junk. Tiny paws skittered in the shadows. He could feel beady little eyes watching him. He paused inside the maze, in what he supposed was the middle of the living room. He'd known hoarders in his time—his grandmother had collected china figurines—but this was one for the books. Suddenly uneasy, he considered turning back, calling it quits. But then the needle tracks on his arms began to itch—the monkey on his back reminding him why he was here—and so he scratched his arms and continued looking.

He couldn't see a TV anywhere. If the crazy old bat even owned a TV, it was most likely broken and piled somewhere with all her other broken TV sets. He briefly wondered if any of this shit was antique—but where to even begin looking? "Stupid old bitch," he grumbled; when he robbed someone's house, at the very least he expected they have something worth stealing. There was nothing here for him, he decided. Wasn't even worth looking upstairs.

Vern was about to turn around and shuffle back down the aisle, careful not to disturb the perilous towers of junk, when he saw something gleaming. A large jewelled brooch in the shape of a bird—a crow, Vern thought at first—perched upon a pile of dusty TV guides. The bird was feathered with glittering black and white stones, with sparkling red eyes, and yellow claws. Had to be worth a fortune.

Vern snatched the jewelled bird as if afraid it would fly away. It was stuck to the pile of magazines. He gave a fierce tug, and something twanged loudly like a broken guitar string. There was a pause, before the room began to rumble and quake as if a subway train was passing beneath the house, and the towers of junk began to shudder ominously. Vern frowned at the brooch in his hand. It wasn't a crow, he suddenly realised. It was a magpie, the thief of the avian world. And there was a length of fishing line—now a broken length of fishing line—attached to the back of it.

The towers of junk swayed above him like snakes above a mouse, cloaking him in shadow. Vern glanced along the aisle towards the living room door. Attached to the back of it was a cracked mirror in which he saw his reflection, wearing a look of resigned dread like Wile E. Coyote in the Roadrunner cartoons. The door suddenly seemed far away. Too far to run before…

The first tower fell, collapsing across the aisle in front of Vern and crashing into the tower directly opposite, creating a domino effect, a Mexican Wave of junk that whirlpooled around him—before it all came crashing down.

A thick cloud of dust mushroomed above the rubble. Startled mice skittered about the debris like the survivors of a natural disaster. And from somewhere deep inside the great mound of trash came Vern's weak, wheezy whimper.

When Mrs. Fogle returned home later that evening, and saw that someone had broken in, she set down her bag—which was swollen with all the treasure she'd collected that day—and surveyed the damage in the living room.

She pursed her lips, gave a fussy little shake of her head, and then she set about tidying the mess, rearranging her treasure just the way she liked it.

A place for everything, and everything in its place.

At last, she found Vern buried beneath the piles of treasure, squished like a bug under a fly—swat. "Not again," she sighed.

Mrs. Fogle gave another fussy little shake of her head, prised the jewelled magpie brooch from his stiff, clawed hand; and then she went and put Vern with the others.

ೞ✠ഝ

Adam Howe *is an English writer of screenplays and fiction. Writing as Garrett Addams, his short story Jumper was chosen by Stephen King as the winner of the On Writing contest. His fiction has appeared or is scheduled to appear in* Nightmare Magazine, Horror Library Volume 5, Beware the Dark, Of Devils & Deviants: An Anthology of Erotic Horror, *and* Bete Noire issues 7 & 10. *Tweet him @Adam_G_Howe.*

The Masque of Medico

Florence Grey

The Masque—Medico della Peste—
Looking under crystalline spectacles to show
The pain hidden beneath,
Windows of the soul, black as death around the eyes
From the funeral pyre.
 "In all thy works be mindful of thy last end, and thou will never sin again."
Porcelain perfection to hide the twisted, perverted beauty
Smelling of roses, mint, spices, and camphor to shun the
Apocaplytic miasma of God's Carnival.
   Momento mori…remember your mortality.

Florence Grey *has been writing poetry for nearly twenty years. She loves the swing and big band era and prefers writing her poetry with pen and paper to that of a computer.*

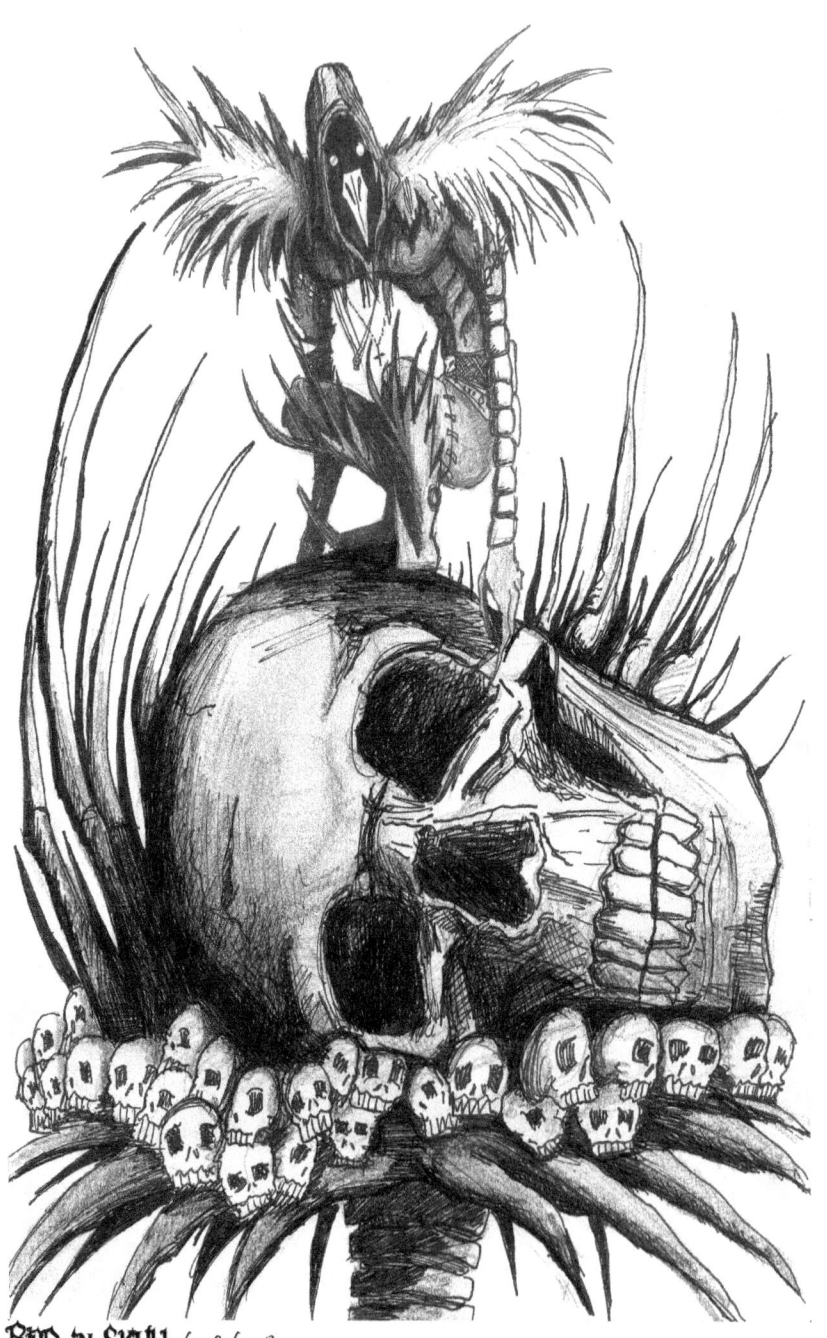

BIRD 'N SKULL *by Luke Spooner*

Luke Spooner *a.k.a. 'Carrion House' currently lives and works in the South of England. Having recently graduated from the University of Portsmouth with a first class degree he is now a full time illustrator for just about any project that peaks his interest. Despite regular forays into children's books and fairy tales his true love lies in anything macabre, melancholy or dark in nature and essence. He believes that the job of putting someone else's words into a visual form, to accompany and support their text, is a massive responsibility as well as being something he truly treasures.*

www.carrionhouse.com
www.facebook.com/carrionhouse

A Theory of Unremarkable Madness

J. J. Steinfeld

> GARCIN: Hell is...other people.
> — No Exit (Huis Clos), Jean-Paul Sartre (1905-1980)

> JAQUES: All the world's a stage,
> And all the men and women merely players;
> They have their exits and their entrances...
> — As You Like It, Act II, Scene vii, William Shakespeare (1564-1616)

As he walked quickly down the hallway of his high school, English teacher Eugene Howell, looking at the first page of a student's thirty-page short story on time travel which he had marked throughout in red pen where he thought it had been plagiarized, bumped with considerable force into a student, the pages of the short story scattering as he fell to the floor before realizing who the student was: Zachary Drusmire, the seventeen-year-old author of the short story. Eugene's right hand and watch banged hard against a student locker before he hit the floor even harder. It felt as though he had run into a bruising linebacker on the football team, not the basketball team's skinny point guard.

Zachary, wearing a lovely tweed sport coat and fancy silk tie, much nicer and more expensive than his sport coat and tie, Eugene thought, started to help his English teacher up but the man brushed away the assistance. Eugene found it difficult to believe that this skinny not all that tall young man was the star of the school's basketball team. The teacher, barely a six-footer, was a good two inches taller than Zachary. Eugene remembered trying out for his high-school basketball team, nearly forty years ago, and being the first one cut. He hated that memory and tried to block it out, but it persistently clawed at him.

"Remember, our meeting is for three o'clock. I will see you and your father then in the vice-principal's office," Eugene said to his student, as he began to pick up the sheets of paper. "Try to be on time," he added, looking at his injured right wrist, his old watch, which he had worn throughout his thirty years of teaching, now broken.

"Our meeting doesn't bother me at all," Zachary said in a strong, confident voice, picking up five pages of his short story, smiling with satisfaction at his work despite his teacher's critical markings. "But I did have a horrible dream last night that the world ended precisely at three o'clock. Strange how the subconscious works sometimes."

"Even the end of the world isn't going to let you off the hook."

"That is my short story, every word of it, Mr. Howell."

"Your short story with help from the immortal H. G. Wells, I'd say."

"My short story pays homage to H. G. Wells. Wells, in his day, had to deal with accusations of plagiarism also."

"Thirty pages of dubious writing, Zachary…"

Thirty pages. Thirty years as a high-school English teacher. The number *thirty* slapped at Eugene's mind. He suddenly recalled that today was the deadline for applying for early retirement. He had been thinking about it all semester, for the last two years actually. He'd be fifty-five before the end of the school year. Over half of his life as a high-school English teacher, that was long enough, he decided. He could e-mail the application in before five o'clock, right after the meeting. *Don't forget*, he warned himself.

"Besides, your Wellsian story is much too long, Zachary. The assignment was for no more than two-thousand words…absolute maximum."

"The story's flow dictated its length, Mr. Howell. My fingers were dancing on the keyboard. Exactly seven thousand six hundred and eighty-three glorious words. I didn't even have to do a second draft."

"You channelling H. G. Wells?"

"I'm not channelling anyone, past or present, Mr. Howell."

"You are not H. G. Wells in the past. You are a high-school student in the present." Eugene believed his student's short story was taken from an early version of a H. G. Wells short story, perhaps portions of an early draft of Wells' novel *The Time Machine* the student had somehow located, even if the teacher couldn't track down the source on the internet. Eugene in his sleuthing had discovered that an earlier incarnation of the novel had first been published as a short story called "The Chronic Argonauts" in a school journal when H. G. Wells was in his early twenties, but that short story, which he read on the internet, wasn't incriminating enough. Perhaps an even earlier version of "The Chronic Argonauts" existed, if he could track it down.

"That horrible dream of mine was awfully vivid."

"Please be on time, regardless of the planet's status."

Zachary smiled with an easy-going charm and said he had never been late for anything in his life. "My father taught me punctuality is indicative of good character." Eugene had a shiver of distress. He'd been late to several meetings and functions lately, even forgetting to go to one altogether. The application for early retirement, he had to get it in today, five o'clock at the latest.

Eugene had seen Zachary's father the other day on television, an amazingly large man who seemed to fill the entire screen, promoting a graphic novel he had written and illustrated: *The Wonder of The Unearthly Wonder*. He couldn't believe that this four-hundred-fifty-pound professional wrestler, The Unearthly Wonder, and Zachary were actually father and son. Perhaps Zachary took after his mother, who Eugene had been told by the vice-principal had remarried and moved away before Zachary had started high school last year.

"This is very serious, young man," Eugene said.

"No one is denying the gravity of your accusation," Zachary said, and smiled with even more charm. "See you at three o'clock. Time is of the essence, as my father says," the student said and laughed.

"What's so funny?" Eugene asked as the student walked away. The teacher's wrist seemed to be hurting even more. He shook his watch, trying to bring it back to life.

"The absurdity of the high-school experience," Zachary called back, without turning around, then pantomiming dribbling a basketball and making an imaginary jump shot.

Eugene hurried to the staff room but had trouble opening its door using his right hand, but after some twisting and pulling of the doorknob with his left hand, managed to open the door. He entered the newly renovated staff room and slammed the door shut behind him, apologizing for the noise to the other five teachers already there — teachers in science, history, math, physical education, a second English teacher — and immediately went to the coffee-and-tea-making table.

Glancing at the clock above the table, Eugene put Zachary's short story down and started to pour himself a cup of coffee. "This isn't the right time, is it?" he said, the pain in his injured hand worsening as he prepared his coffee.

"It was the correct time when I came in," Donna Gallagher, the science teacher said, checking her wristwatch.

"Looks like it stopped," Tony Eddings, the physical-education teacher and the school's basketball coach, said.

"It's sped up. I came in at twelve-nineteen and now it's twelve-forty, and I haven't been here more than three minutes," Eugene claimed.

"My watch says twelve-forty-three, but it always seems to be fast," Melvin Richardson, the math teacher, said.

"Twelve-forty-one…and my watch never misses a beat," the science teacher said.

"I've only been in her for three lousy minutes," Eugene emphasized, and spilled some coffee on Zachary's short story as he stirred. The stains made several of the pages look as though they were Rorschach inkblot tests.

"Your memory is playing tricks with you, Eugene."

Eugene admitted he had been forgetting things lately, some of them little, not all that significant, but other things he had attempted to recall were important, at least to him and his past.

"Forgetting, regrettably, goes hand-in-hand with the ageing process," the other English teacher, Claudia Kaplansky, who had been teaching film and drama all semester, said, preparing a coffee as she stood next to Eugene. She had a copy of Sartre's *No Exit* with her and sat down in a large chair near the room's only window to read as she drank her coffee. Eugene recalled that she had brought the same play to the staff room at the beginning of the school year and was pleased with the sharpness of his memory in this instance, but frustrated he couldn't recall its title in French. Zachary Drusmire had used several French phrases in his short story; in fact, phrases from several different languages. That was what had made Eugene initially suspect the essay had been plagiarized. That, and the style and brilliance of the short story. Eugene wondered if Claudia remembered that he had asked her out for a drink that day, confiding in her that his marriage was in a shambles. She turned him down by saying colleagues should never date, especially if one or both were vulnerable.

Eugene picked up the coffee-stained short story and walked to the chair next to Claudia's. "At three I have a meeting with Zachary Drusmire's father and the vice-principal."

"I've seen him wrestle. Hope he doesn't lift you over his head, Eugene, and twirl you into oblivion. That wouldn't do your teaching career any good," the other English teacher said.

Teaching career, Eugene thought, the two words caught in a web of mockery and irony and painful self-doubt. He hadn't told anyone in the room he had been contemplating early retirement, that his attachment to teaching was growing more tenuous each day he entered the classroom.

"What did Zachary do?" asked the science teacher.

"Plagiarism or breaking my wrist and watch, take your pick," Eugene said, holding up his injured wrist and broken watch for everyone in the staff room to see.

"He attacked you, Eugene?"

"No, it was an accident. More my fault, but the plagiarism is upsetting," Eugene explained. He looked again at his broken watch and threw it into a nearby wastebasket, conducting some sort of hasty funeral rite.

"Great three-pointer there," the physical-education teacher remarked.

"He's an exceptionally bright kid," the other English teacher defended the high-school student.

"He couldn't have written this short story," Eugene said to Claudia, to everyone in the staff room, but most of all to himself.

The PA crackled forth a short message that no one in the staff room understood.

"When are they going to fix that idiotic PA system?" Eugene said, looking up at the intercom speaker.

"Sounds louder than before," the math teacher commented.

"What language is that in? It's not French, is it?"

The other five teachers offered their guesses: Spanish ... Italian ... Russian ... Japanese ... Pig Latin ...

"You're not being serious, are you?" Eugene said to all the teachers in the staff room.

"It's hard to make out, but it did sound like Pig Latin to me," the math teacher said.

"Sounds like Zachary's voice. You think he's hacked into the intercom system?" Eugene asked.

"It's the vice-principal's. Higher pitched than Zachary's," the science teacher said.

A few minutes later there was a message about not smoking anywhere on school grounds that changed halfway through into gibberish.

"You think Zachary has supernatural powers? His father is The Unearthly Wonder, isn't he?" Lauren Raymill, the history teacher, said.

"Speaking of supernatural, unearthly powers, I'll never forget his stunning book report on *The Midwich Cuckoos* last year, comparing the novel to the film *Village of the Damned*, the original 1960 version. Zachary gave an oral presentation in which he argued that *Village of the Damned* was the greatest science-fiction film adaptation of a novel," the other English teacher said. "I wish I could have gotten that presentation on video. I swear, it was as scary as the novel or the film."

"I remember him writing on a test that he created this school and we're all characters in his play. He's the writer and director...and the star," Eugene disclosed.

"All the world's a stage, Shakespeare wrote."

"Who doesn't know that," Eugene snapped back, feeling as though his memory was being questioned.

"What play, act, and scene?"

"We've not on some TV quiz show, are we?"

"I think Zachary was being facetious and playful, Eugene."

The history teacher gave her own Zachary Drusmire the brilliant-student story: "His last two history essays were on Julius and Ethel Rosenberg and on Sacco and Venzetti. I don't think any of the other students even knew who they were and he gave the most moving class presentations. That would make another captivating if not educational video."

"Am I the only one that doesn't buy into the perfect-student myth of Zachary Drusmire?" Eugene said, and unsuccessfully attempted to make a cellphone call to the vice-principal. "It's those high-voltage electrical towers outside the school."

"We've used our cellphones in here before the renovations," the math teacher pointed out.

"Zachary mentions them in his story," Eugene said, finding the place in the story: "He calls them prodigious and Brobdingnagian... iconic...precursors of cataclysmic occurrences."

"At least he's being creative," the other English teacher said.

"That's not the parts he plagiarized from H. G. Wells. Zachary claims the high-voltage electrical towers affect cognition and memory," Eugene said, and found a section in the short story describing their mind-affecting hazards.

"I had Zachary in my class last year. He was the best student writer I ever had."

"He couldn't have written this short story. Not possible..."

The math teacher said, "He's a whiz at math. I think he's better at calculus than I am. The kid should be in college, not high school."

The science teacher, as if presenting a legal argument, said, "He built the sweetest-looking time-machine model for advanced-science class."

"Did he take a ride in it?"

"A model made out of plywood and pieces of metal, with cute little beeping sounds. Not the most sophisticated special effects, but impressive all the same."

"You can't get the kid suspended," the physical-education teacher said.

"If he plagiarized," Eugene insisted.

"Big game next week. He's physically amazing. Smallest kid on the team and he can slam dunk. Heck, our starting centre can't even slam dunk."

"If he admits he plagiarized his short story," Eugene said, starting to put the sheets of the story back in order, "and is willing to write a new story from scratch, then I will give him another chance."

"Look at the time. It keeps changing. Definitely some weird electrical malfunction," the history teacher said.

"The high-voltage contraptions or maybe the wiring got messed up during the renovations," Eugene speculated.

The PA crackled forth again.

"What language is that?" Eugene shouted.

The math teacher went to open the door and said, "The lock is jammed."

"My cellphone isn't working either," the history teacher said.

"Someone should be coming here to get us out," the science teacher chuckled.

"Sartre's *No Exit*," the other English teacher said, and held up the book.

"Just relax. We'll hear the next period's bell. Forget the clock."

Eugene walked to the window, looking out at the school grounds and the high-voltage electrical towers in the distance: "Is it illogical to ask someone to list the ten most important things they've ever forgotten?" The other five teachers in the room looked puzzled.

"If remembered, do they qualify for the list and why compile lists on such a benevolent day?" Eugene explained by way of another question, feeling he was speaking to some of his students.

"Who calls weather *benevolent*?" the history teacher in the room said.

"I can't think of a better word than *benevolent* to describe today's gorgeous weather," Eugene defended himself.

"Benevolent until you turn on the radio or read the newspaper," the history teacher said, rolling up the newspaper he had been reading and jabbing Eugene lightly in the stomach.

"I'd sure like to forget some things and remember others, but life and my brain don't seem to work that way," the math teacher said.

"Later in life, I question if we can remember the names of a fraction of the teachers we had in school? Try making a list of all the teachers you ever had and see how many you can come up with," the science teacher challenged. Then she slowly poured the remainder of her tea into the sink as if she were pouring out old memories and began to make himself a fresh cup.

Eugene wanted to tell the other English teacher that he wished he had the memory of them as lovers. He had dreamed about them together on several occasions, and recalled them all clearly. But what was the title of *No Exit* in French? He poured himself another coffee.

"Maybe we should try compiling a list of all our old flames and heartthrobs," the history teacher added, theatrically clasping his hands over his heart.

"I think the heart has a better memory than the head," the math teacher argued.

"You're getting more romantic in your dotage," the science teacher said, throwing a mocking kiss at the math teacher.

"Memory is very complex. We arrange and rearrange our words and thoughts, hiding some, cherishing others. There are so many levels of remembering. What about the ethical choices you faltered with? Moral decisions you fouled up?" Eugene said, wishing he and the other English teacher were somewhere else together.

"You should teach philosophy," the math teacher said.

"I have come to despise teaching. I don't blame the students but it is not my calling any longer," Eugene said with a harsh expression and then he smiled, as if attempting to erase his disheartening words.

"They are too young for *No Exit* or I'd teach it. In the words of Garcon, 'Hell is…other people,'" the other English teacher said.

"Hell is teaching in this school," Eugene said with a smile, looking for a favourable reaction from Claudia.

"Why don't you switch careers?" the math teacher said.

"I'm considering taking early retirement," Eugene revealed.

"You're a good teacher," the history teacher consoled him.

"Not by my standards," Eugene said.

The other English teacher looked up from her book and said, "I wonder if I'd get fired for inappropriate dress…and behaviour. Sometimes I have an urge to dress up as the quintessential tart and walk

into the vice-principal's office, tell her I think this would be more con-
ducive for learning, at least for the boys. Sometimes it is difficult to get
them to pay attention."

To Eugene's astonishment, first the history teacher left the staff
room, joking that she didn't know which room she was supposed to
teach her next class in, followed by the science teacher, who joked that
Zachary's time machine would take her back to a better day, then the
math and physical-education teachers left, hitting each other in the
arms like two playful schoolboys, and Eugene was relieved the other
English teacher remained in her chair.

"I really thought they wouldn't get the door open."

"They were teasing you, Eugene. You need some cheeriness in your
sombre life."

Eugene went to the door and tried it once more: "It's stuck again."

"We'll get it open."

Eugene walked over to the woman and asked her if she'd like to
have a drink with him tonight. "You could dress any way you wish,"
he said, and offered a gentle smile of longing, hoping he didn't appear
lecherous in any way.

"Are you divorced yet?" she asked, looking at the play.

"We've been separated since school started and now it's almost
ended, and we're still separated."

"Hope you work things out," she said. "Last time I went out with a
married man, and technically you are still married, Eugene, it turned
into a fiasco."

Eugene returned to the coffee-and-tea-making table. There must be
an easier way to stay out of Hell, he thought, and pushed over the coffee maker, but already starting an apology before it hit the floor. Then,
as he picked up the broken coffee maker, he said the play title *Huis
Clos* loudly and joyously, as if attempting to wake a class of sleeping
students.

The clock was at five minutes to three. "That's ludicrous. Everyone
had a different time. Those high-voltage electrical towers. I've never
trusted them. Look at the size of them. We've lost two hours."

"No we haven't, Eugene. Malfunctions, that's all."

"I have an important meeting to get to."

"It isn't three o'clock yet."

"It is! It is!"

Eugene could see The Unearthly Wonder lumbering toward the
building and his son, Zachary, on the front steps by the entrance, wav-
ing to his father. Eugene closed his eyes and could imagine Zachary
and his father sitting in the vice-principal's office, waiting for him to

arrive, The Unearthly Wonder declaring that punctuality is indicative of good character. Eugene feared they would discuss his teaching career, make accusations against him, condemn *him.*

"This window is stuck!" he yelled.

"Please try to calm down," the other English teacher said, and left the room, no longer wanting to be near her erratically behaving colleague.

Not long afterward, as loud knocking turned to pounding at the door, Eugene, his wrist inflamed with pain, was still attempting to open the window, so he could escape…and make it to the three o'clock meeting. He knew if he made it to the meeting on time, all the little disruptions to his mind would be smoothed out. After the meeting, he told himself, he would buy a new watch.

Canadian poet, fiction writer, and playwright J. J. Steinfeld *lives on Prince Edward Island, where he is patiently waiting for Godot's arrival and a phone call from Kafka. While waiting, he has published fourteen books, including* Should the Word Hell Be Capitalized? *(Stories, Gaspereau Press),* Would You Hide Me? *(Stories, Gaspereau Press),* An Affection for Precipices *(Poetry, Serengeti Press),* Misshapenness *(Poetry, Ekstasis Editions),* Word Burials *(Novel and Stories, Crossing Chaos Enigmatic Ink), and* A Glass Shard and Memory *(Stories, Recliner Books). More than three hundred of his short stories and nearly six hundred poems have appeared in anthologies and periodicals internationally, and over forty of his one-act plays and a handful of full-length plays have been performed in Canada and the United States.*

Countess Bathory's Procurer

Marge Simon

My lady was a saint beyond question,
of this I am sure, yet with certain needs
while her husband served his king.
To these, I willingly attended.

He returned, ill from war and wounds
that never healed. I withdrew, pursued
my own designs with herbal pouch and
promises to salve the broken hearts
of sweet young girls, never dreaming
Erzebet would be the victim.

And so I doomed my Countess Bathory.
Thruzo's men found one girl dead, others
drained of blood, they claimed, to furnish
her with milky skin and youth. All lies!
My lady had no need for virgin blood.
She bathed in water; I chose otherwise.

It saddened me when bricks were laid
one by one in solid rows, the mortar firmed:
a wall to keep her in her cell, to keep me out,
but of our liaison, she never told.

ೞ✠ೞ

Marge Simon's *works appear in publications such as* Strange Horizons, Niteblade, DailySF Magazine, Pedestal Magazine, Dreams & Night-mares. *She edits a column for the HWA Newsletter and serves as Chair of the Board of Trustees. She has won the Strange Horizons Readers Choice Award, the Bram Stoker Award™(2008, 2012), the Rhysling Award and the Dwarf Stars Award. Collections:* Like Birds in the Rain, Unearthly De-lights, The Mad Hattery, Vampires, Zombies & Wanton Souls, *and* Dangerous Dreams. Member HWA, SFWA, SFPA. *www.margesimon.com*

A-Haunting We Will Go

Fred L. Taulbee, Jr.

I saw the man I had just murdered running down the stairs as I and twelve others entered the subway train. I sat down on a bench just opposite the doors. I breathed deeply, satisfied at a job well done once again, and looked around at the usual people sitting and standing around me on the train.

The doors were still open and the man I had just murdered was going to make the train and I was glad. We had much to talk about. There was no doubt he was dead. There was never a doubt. I had planned it well. The dark slit at his throat was still there, widening and closing as he ran, and the blood that issued forth a few moments before now soaked his clothes. The suit jacket was dark so the blood didn't show as much there. But the blood had soaked the white button-up shirt so that it'd be hard to guess the shirt had ever been white. Even the tie I had cut as a jibe, a joke, was still there at his neck more like a bowtie now. I laughed under my breath. I never thought while killing him that seeing his tie like that would make me want to laugh so hard. Maybe it was just the release of all that pressure, a place to put the leftover adrenaline afterward.

I looked away as he entered. He was actually panting. I watched him out of the corner of my eye, ignoring him as if I couldn't see him. The train started, and he jerked with it, but a little bit late, as if he was only doing it because he thought it should have that effect on him in his new state.

He ran his hands over his shirt and felt his neck, as if he had already come to the realization that he was dead and was just doublechecking. Then he diddled with what was left of his tie, and I laughed under my breath but loud enough for him to hear.

He looked at me with surprise on his face. I tried to stop laughing, but I just couldn't. The joke—pretending I couldn't see him—was up, so I raised my head, stopped laughing and just smiled at him.

He looked around at the other twelve passengers, moved closer and whispered, "You killed me."

I continued his low tones, "Yes."

"I'm definitely dead."

"Of course. I wasn't about to screw this up."

He kept touching his body. It seemed so arbitrary. If he wanted to test out his corporeal-ness or lack thereof why didn't he just knock on his head, snap his fingers or dance a jig?

"You planned this? You're some kind of murderer?"

I sang the last sentence lightly to the tune of "You're Some Kind of Wonderful."

I laughed. He did not.

He whispered again, looking around at the others, "You're insane."

The smile dropped from my face. What should I say to that? Have I not thought that a million times myself? I never denied it. But this time was different—wasn't it?

He saw my suddenly-serious look and sensed a speech coming so he kept quiet, and I continued in a kind of yelling whisper that others could probably hear but ignored anyway.

"Me? Insane?"

"Yes, you, insane," he answered.

"If I killed someone and that makes me a murderer, then what are you?"

The guilt colored his face red, and it was genuine shock. He really never knew what was up. He never suspected a thing. But I'm not talking about his murder, the one that just occurred three blocks away. I'm talking about another one.

"Sarah."

"What?"

It wasn't really a question. It was one of those stall words like "uhm" or "dude." Most of the time we're just filling in the vocals while we think. Other times, times like these, guilt makes attempt some kind of surreptitious stammer.

"Don't pretend you don't know what I'm talking about. But I'll remind you. You killed your wife, and I know all about it."

New shock on his face. The man was capable of so many different shades of red.

I went on. "You were clever. Well done indeed. You left some blood here and there, but I cleaned it up for you. You left the parts in different places, but that wasn't really necessary. The disguise you used wasn't bad—I'm so glad you didn't try a mask or fake facial hair—your mannerisms were still noticeable, but no problem. I deleted the footage from the three security cameras that caught you leaving the scene of the crime, when you were supposedly in Las Vegas. And your alibis in Las Vegas weren't that good. I mean, come on. An Angelino is always going to use Vegas as an alibi, but they have even more cameras there.

"But no worries. While pretending to be you, I signed your name into the physical log of a Vegas motel that didn't have cameras. Plus, they used a simple software program for their registration, so it was easy to go to a past date and add your name. You paid cash by the way. Traces of your DNA from the real crime scene are at this motel—well, that covers everything. If I missed anything, it's circumstantial enough so that you would not have had to worry about it.

He wasn't believing me, but that didn't matter.

"You should ask why I did all that, why I covered your ass."

He almost gave in and asked, but I kept talking.

"I am a troubled man," I explained.

I looked down, seriously thinking about how troubled I was, and then realized how melodramatic it seemed. When I looked back up, he had an expression as if he agreed with my claim of being troubled.

I continued. I knew he had killed his wife and that was a surprise to him. But I had more. "I liked the way the sun hit her hair sometimes, all golden with natural colors, as if you could see a reflection of the sun in her hair."

His face questioned me, but he knew what I was talking about.

"She always smelled good."

His face told me more now. He knew I was talking about Sarah.

"You see, I have allergies, and my sense of smell is weak, but if someone puts on just a little bit extra of the right undaunting perfume it really gets my attention."

"Were you stalking my wife?"

I ignored his question.

"The way her breastbone kind of protruded from all of her years in ballet class."

"How long were you stalking her?"

I stood up and said, "I wasn't stalking her, you fool."

I stood and paced the train car, hovering unnecessarily close to the others who were ignoring both of us. I leaned against a pole a few feet from him and continued in a low voice. "You remember three years ago, when you started cheating on her?"

He worked hard not to change his expression. I calmed down a bit.

"That's when I met Sarah. I met her at the grocery store. Classic hook up really. I mean, I never thought I'd meet someone at a grocery store, but I always tried to go around five-thirty or six, after everybody gets off work and picks up groceries."

Still, he had that same expression, as if he were trying not to look flabbergasted.

"Yeah, she had three bottles of merlot in her cart, along with some bread and dipping oil and those garlic-stuffed olives."

The merlot, bread and oil did nothing to him, but when I mentioned the garlic-stuffed olives his face dropped. I don't know why. It's all Mediterranean food, but he didn't realize this.

"You could've just been stalking her and saw all that in her cart."

"You idiot. I already told you about the ballet thing. That should be enough. I wish I could tell you something that would tell you for sure like where her birthmark was, but she didn't have one."

Another layer of unbelievability left his face. Now, I felt I could confess everything to him. I sat down and stared out at the black walls zooming by. I waved him closer, but he didn't move until I nodded towards the others in the car, trying not bother them.

"I had seen her wedding ring in the grocery store, but I thought to myself, 'what the hell?' We talked. I must've met her right when she found out you were cheating on her, right when a person comes to the decision of leaving a person, or expanding their own choices. And after a few weeks of talking, she decided we should date. We dated for a year and a half."

I looked up at him.

"I can see by your expression that we did a good job of keeping it from you. We were careful. For every ten affairs found out there's one done right. Just like murder. Some don't get caught because there is no sign. We deleted texts, deleted recent calls, deleted emails, cleared browser histories, deleted each other from social networks and then refriended up, regular doctor appointments, lunch dates, and careful planning around your careless planning. For a while it was our tit for your tat, like not just instant karma, but simultaneous karma. John Lennon would like that."

Now he knew I knew her, but he still wasn't sure the affair was true.

"You claim you had an affair with my wife, and then you killed me because I—you think I—killed her?"

"Good, good. You're keeping up. She said you weren't so sharp, but you're doing fine. "

He rolled his eyes, and I continued explaining.

"She changed me. I never knew anybody could love me. I never knew I could love anybody. I was mad, angry at everything all the time. If I had killed everybody I seriously thought about killing I would've already been in the history books and the gas chamber. I had moments of clarity, and I had one that first day Sarah and I met, and I focused on staying that way even when we weren't together. And I got better. You see, I have problems you don't even want to know about."

He wasn't interested in my problems.

"We did everything together. We took dance lessons, went wine tasting, watched movies—all the stuff that people in a normal relationship do. I bought her flowers all the time. She'd take pictures of them, but she'd keep them at my house. Sometimes she'd take one flower and press it into a book or something.

"What happened with you two?"

It was a genuine question. Maybe the story got to him, maybe he was curious about his wife, maybe he was vying for time. Methinks, the latter. And he doubled up with another question.

"Was she happy? "

"Yes. She was, most of the time. She wasn't happy when she talked about you, but when she got you off her mind she was peacefully happy."

"What happened?"

"Hell, I guess."

He wasn't sure what I meant, but it wasn't supposed to be clear.

"She started worrying about her soul. She thought she was going to hell because she was cheating on you. So she broke it off. And after a few weeks of agnostic me trying to change her mind, I realized I just wanted her to be happy. "

He nodded his head here, as if that was all he wanted also, and this coming from the man who killed her.

"It was hard on me. The phone calls stopped. Then the emails stopped. I held on for the next few years with the acceptance that I had experienced something wonderful, and should just be happy to have experienced it, even if it weren't forever."

He nodded again, as if he knew what I was talking about, just a couple of killers being human.

"I'm just sorry I wasn't there in time to stop you," I said. "I watched her as often as possible. I think she knew. Sometimes she would move her rearview mirror around to every angle and then straighten it back. When she was shopping she would sometimes stop and look into the windows at the reflections. Sometimes I would let her see me, smile at her and quietly walk away, as if I were just passing by.

He looked out the train as if reflecting upon this himself.

"I dug up the parts you buried in all the different places, and I buried her in a cemetery between two graves, and carefully hid all signs of it. Only I know where she rests."

This pissed him off for some reason, but it faded, changing to something else, as if he had something to tell me, so I waited for it as I looked around at the other passengers.

He ran his palms down his chest, verifying the obvious, that he was dead, and then looked over at me.

"I'm going to make you pay for killing me."

I said nothing, and tried a lax expression, a poker face.

He looked around at the others and whispering and yelling at the same time he began, "This is what I'm going to do. I don't know how this works, but I'm here with you. I can follow you, probably wherever you go." He paused for dramatic effect. "I'm going to haunt you for the rest of your life. I'm going to learn everything I need to know about this world, and I'm going to haunt you. I'm going to remind you of Sarah every day. I'm going to torment you like you've never been tormented before. You thought you were a troubled man before. Wait till I get done with you.

Then he lunged at me and swung — this was what he was vying time for. He was making plans. But I knew what would happen, so I didn't flinch as his fist went through my head without raising a hair on my neck.

When he recovered from his swing, but not his disappointment, I said in a louder voice, "Look around."

He didn't. He just looked at me.

"Look around," I told him again, but he still wouldn't, so I continued. I spoke in normal tones so those around could hear. "It's an afternoon train. All the eight to fivers aren't here yet. And it's a weekday, so the kids haven't gotten out of school yet. But this car is full."

I pointed to the door between the cars. "Look through there. That car has one person in it. This one has twelve people in it, besides you and I, a nice even dozen. I always wanted a nice baker's dozen. I always knew there'd be one more. Thirteen, such a magical number, not like the goody two shoes, three and seven, but a more serious magic number, a mature one that doesn't belong in Disney fairy tales, just horror stories, the real fairy tales. Yeah, I'm a troubled man. But Sarah, she calmed me. She made me not want to kill."

He looked confused.

I laughed. I ran up and turned a late twenties man around. "This is the man who tried to mug me, and while he didn't make me want to kill again, I certainly had the desire to do so.

I pointed to a beautiful young girl, "This is a girl I met at a bar who tried to roll me and then missed me with her tazer. This is a bum who was already dying of a hit and run. Here is a man with road rage for me, and who started taking it out on his woman—that's when I started following my prey."

I ran over to three Latinos. "Over here we have a trio of wannabe gangsters, terrorizing people, robbing people—I egged them on, made it look like self defense just for my own peace of mind."

I ran over to a very thin and sore-ridden man and woman. "Here we have a couple of drug addicts who had been robbing little old ladies— that's when I decided to become self-righteous and kill those who deserved it more, such as this guy, an old man molesting a teenage girl, and this guy, a man spreading std's on purpose, and this old lady who killed dogs but had a hundred cats, and then over there we have just a regular asshole, much like my latest.

As they were introduced each person turned around reluctantly toward him. Each one had been killed the same way, slashed through the throat. The blood had drenched each of them the same way, except that none of them made me laugh as much as seeing his cut tie like a bowtie.

"You see, I don't know how this works either. Hell, I'm agnostic, but really I'm closer to atheist. So this old hell thing—I don't really believe in it anymore than heaven. But based on my experience with my friends here, my victims as some might say, well," and I got close to his face, "It's me who is haunting them, and it's me who will be haunting you."

He had nothing to say.

"I don't know what it is. Maybe you and all of them are in limbo. Or maybe you are supposed to be haunting me, and all of you just suck at it, or maybe this is hell for you. Maybe Sarah was right about that. But yeah, it's me who will be haunting you till the day I die, and I might even haunt you after that too. I don't know."

The girl who tried to roll and taze me, approached him first, "Help me. Get me out of here, please."

The pathetic drug addicts and the wife-beating road-rager, all claimed their innocence and begged him to help them.

The wannabe gangsters approached him as the others backed up. They circled him, pushed him around. They liked to play along. And it was fun to watch. I couldn't touch him or any of them, so it was always nice to see some of them do my haunting for me.

The others said nothing, resigned to their hells.

He said nothing. There was a look in his eye. His face changed. Went lax. Like when somebody realizes something and finally accepts it, as if he had taken a deep breath and gotten all Buddhist on me. But if he was anything like the others, he'd go crazy with or without my help, but man, was he going to get my help. And the thing I saw in his eyes was Sarah staring back at him from somewhere, Sarah in his head, Sarah on his mind, Sarah, Sarah, Sarah, Sarah, on his mind, in his head, like she was in mine. She would be in my mind until the day I died and hopefully longer.

Fred L. Taulbee Jr. *has been teaching English for seven years, and earned an MA in Literature in 1994 and an MFA in Creative Writing in 2004. He spent the summer of 2013 updating his blogs on teaching and writing, and starting new blogs on poetry and book reviews. His other horror works include a short story "The Flesh is Not Weak" and the novel* House of the Matriarch, *which can be found on Smashwords.com and at most eBook retailers.*

BLIND MAN'S BLUFF

Brian G. Ross

Puffs of grey slid across the night sky, like smoke from an old man's pipe. The moon was full and sat boldly in the black. Celestial bodies twinkled, even through the soup of fog that curled around the hilltops, and fat flakes fluttered in the wind.

Somewhere below all of that Jerry stopped talking about his divorce because, all of a sudden, Gordon had stopped listening. At the very least, before, he had feigned interest.

Gordon stood on the spot with his lips pursed and his finger to them.

"Do you hear that?" He grabbed Jerry's shoulder.

"Hear what?"

"Sssh! Keep it down." His eyes darted this way and that. The trees wore white coats: Gordon zipped up his. "I think they're getting closer."

Jerry shrugged him off. "Who is?"

"I'm not sure, but they're out there." Gordon rubbed his hands together, cupped them, and blew into them, momentarily relieving the sharp, icy chill. "Can't believe I left my gloves back at the lodge."

Jerry listened. "I can't hear a thing. Now, keep moving. This cold will grab you by the balls if you stand still too long." He started circling the fire they had built, big stick *skooshing* in the snow. When he saw he wasn't stopping, Gordon followed.

As the silence between them went on, the elements became more inclement. The snow was heavier now; the fog, thicker. Clouds hung low, pregnant, and streaked across the sky. The moon was nowhere to be seen where only moments ago it had started down upon them with its omniscient eye.

"I thought you people were supposed to have ears like elephants," he said, catching up.

"What people?"

"You know, blind folk."

Jerry laughed. "You mean, ears like a *dog*."

"Huh?"

"Elephants have *big* ears, but they haven't got better hearing for it. Dogs — now they can hear a fart on the dark side of the moon."

"Whatever."

The wind slapped the trees like an angry lover.

"It's an urban myth anyway," Jerry assured him. "Can't see shit; can't hear nothing either, except you that is." He smiled, throwing it at him like it was an accusation.

"Well I ain't crazy. Sounds like some kind of wild animal."

"Get a grip of yourself, Gordon. It's bad enough we may have to sleep out here without you giving us nightmares as well."

"Christ, I hope not." Gordon stopped and sat on a rock that poked out from the snow, turned up his collar, and pulled his head in like a tortoise. "We'll freeze to death."

"If we're not eaten first."

"Gee, thanks!" He looked at Jerry and, seeing the smile, realised he still possessed that sick sense of humour, even out here, at fifteen below. "The snow came in without warning. I've never seen anything like it."

"Me neither."

This time, either Gordon missed the punchline or chose to ignore it.

"Don't worry," he said. "I called the back-up team. They gave me hell for coming out here in this, but they said they'll be here in two, three hours tops.

"I'm not worried." It was Jerry's turn to stop. He felt around for a resting place of his own. Gordon was about to get up to help him but Jerry found an outcrop with his gloved hand and lowered himself next to the fire. "Calm down. We've got a good fire going. Eddie and the boys will see the smoke and come get us out of here."

"Who are you trying to kid? I can't even see the hand in front of my face."

He tried, wiggling his numb fingers back and forth only inches away from his nose. He could just make out the pale blue skin in the dark fog. He stopped, afraid that if he continued his fingers would drop off one by one into the snow.

Jerry smiled. "Look, just sit down next to the fire and be quiet. Conserve your energy."

"I am sitting down."

"Good."

"What do you mean I should conserve my energy?" Gordon sat on his hands, but there didn't seem to be any heat in his thermal trousers. He put each in turn in his mouth instead, but the sudden temperature change was more painful than soothing. He resorted to hovering them over the flame. "Why the hell aren't you cold?"

"I am."

"You don't look it."

Jerry shifted on his rock and adjusted his glasses. "It's mind over matter, my friend."

As dark as the night was around them, those glasses were a shade more so. His cheeks rode high, a healthy pink; his full lips, pressed together, similarly bright and ripened by a flick of the tongue. His sharp nose blossomed red across the bridge, like a man who has blown it too hard, and a glob of snot hung from its point.

Jerry lifted his nose. "We must be near Cooper's Point." He sensed Gordon's unasked question. "It's in the air."

Gordon felt around for his map, but like them, it was lost. "We can't be at Cooper's Point. When we took off we were nowhere near there."

"Well we're near there now." Again he sniffed.

Gordon forced a laugh. "What? You can *smell* it?"

Jerry nodded. "I told you, it's in the air. I'd say we're about five, maybe ten miles off course." He sniffed the passing wind, like a dog chasing his next meal. "Due east."

"You're having me on." Gordon tried to inhale the night theatrically, but in the company of a blind man he wasn't embarrassed. "I can't smell anything. It's too damn cold."

Jerry was about to say something when the night beat him to it. A sudden rush of wind tore across their makeshift camp and the flame almost danced itself out. After a moment it settled, and beyond the soundtrack of the night, Gordon began to let his imagination get the better of him.

"There." He pointed off into the blizzard, but just as quickly dropped his arm by his side again, realising the futility of it all. "Over there."

"What is it?"

"Don't know, a bear maybe—"

"There's no bears in Scotland."

"—or a wolf—"

"No wolves either," Jerry said, his measured tone countering Gordon's exuberance. "Unless you count werewolves, that is."

"What?"

"I'm just pulling your leg. Christ, you're tighter than my ex-wife."

"Not funny." Gordon hugged himself. "Why the hell did I let you come all the way out here anyway?"

"I don't see how you had a choice in the matter. I'm forty-six years old, and if I want to go hill-climbing, I'll jolly well go hill-climbing. If I want to run naked down Oxford Street, I'll damn well do that too, and there isn't a bloody thing you could do about it." Jerry paused to let the wind get a few words in. "Of course, you didn't have to come with me. Nobody held a gun to your head."

"Yeah well, next time you're on your own."

Jerry leaned forward. "People get lost, whether they have eyes or not." Gordon waved away the attempted profundity and shook his head. "It's nobody's fault," Jerry finished.

"I'm not eight years old anymore. Grown men don't get lost."

"Sure they do. If Christopher Columbus knew where he was going and how to get there, nobody would ever have heard of him."

"How the hell can you get lost going up a mountain?"

"I guess we went left when we should have gone right."

"Huh?"

"Or right when we should have gone left."

"Don't talk stupid," Gordon lambasted. "We're going *up*, right?"

"Yeah."

"So left and right doesn't matter, does it? As long as we're going *up*."

Jerry had to smile at his friend's logic. "Well, whatever way you want to look at it, we *are* lost, that's for sure."

Gordon looked into the blizzard thoughtfully, an intense look of concentration on his face. Trees talked to each other, like old friends. Turning to Jerry, he said, "I think we should get rid of the fire. It attracts too much attention."

"We *want* it to attract attention. How are the guys going to find us without the flame?"

"The wolves will get here before Eddie does, no question." Gordon reached inside his jacket and pulled out his gun. His hand trembled — one part cold, one part fear — and it was all he could do to keep it from falling to the ground.

"Put that thing away, will you? Before you shoot your dick off."

"I won't let them take me without a fight."

Gordon aimed into the black, at nothing, and wondered how close whatever it was that was out there would have to be before he could squeeze off a reliable shot. Feet, perhaps not even that, and by then he knew it would be too late. The longer he held it, the surer he was that a creature was going to jump out of the darkness and devour him right then and there.

Jerry leaned in towards the fire, and the flames licked his face, casting an orange glow upon his skin.

"Do you have any silver bullets in that pea shooter of yours?" he said, his voice low.

The tremor in Gordon's hands had reached his voice. "What the hell are you talking about?"

"For the werewolves. It's the only way to kill them." Jerry touched a finger to the centre of his forehead. "Bang. Right between the eyes."

"But I thought you said—"

Jerry smiled—"Chill", he said— then laughed at his choice of words.

"Right. You're joking. I get it." Gordon popped out the magazine, checked it, then snapped it back in place. "No silver bullets; only got a couple of regulars."

Jerry shook his head. "No good. They'll just bounce right off. May as well toss that away for all the good it'll do."

"How do you know so much about fairy tales, anyway?"

"I used to read a lot back in the day," Jerry said. "But I got too many blisters."

Gordon smiled thinly. "Funny guy."

He looked at his friend's insulated gloves, and wished again that he had remembered to pack his. He rubbed his hands together, trying to generate a little heat, but the cold had sapped his energy, just like Jerry told him it would. He stuck them in his armpits for a quick blast of warmth.

"Sounds like a whole pack of them out there," Jerry piped up.

"I thought you couldn't hear anything?"

"I didn't want to scare you, Gordon. There's a lot of them out there, you know, and they're closer now. Much closer."

"Great." Gordon checked all around him, so fast he thought his head was going to come off his shoulders. "Now you're starting to give me the willies."

"You know, legend has it their noses and ears are so keen, they don't really need their eyes at all."

"Who?"

"Werewolves."

"You can quit the campfire ghost stories, Jerry. It's not funny anymore. Let's just wait for the guys to arrive, all right?"

Jerry looked up from the flame, his eyes now two bright red circles, pulsating behind the dark plastic of his glasses like a heartbeat. He shifted uncomfortably beneath the heavy coat he was wearing, as if his body was trying to escape into the cold.

"What the hell's happening to you?"

Jerry stood up with a fresh enthusiasm. "A wolf's gotta eat. You said yourself, Eddie and the gang won't be here for a couple of hours. You wouldn't want me to go hungry, would you?"

His eyes burned a bolder flame than the one they had struck earlier that night to keep them warm, and now Jerry smiled, his teeth a lot longer and sharper than Gordon remembered.

"But I'm your best friend," Gordon pleaded, moving back. He nearly tripped over his desire to escape.

"Sure you are. Don't worry, buddy. I won't let the others get to you. They'd rip you apart, tear you to pieces, before killing you. They'd make a game out of it. I won't do that to you. I'll make it quick." Jerry took off his glasses and threw them into the fire. The blood red glow grew until it filled the sockets of his eyes. They searched the snow like headlamps. "I promise, you won't feel a thing."

In the distance, further along the ridge, a howl broke the sound of the wind. Gordon headed towards it, on legs that wouldn't run, and with a scream that froze in his throat.

Brian G. Ross *is a thirty-something Australian, based in Scotland. He has over one hundred publications – ranging from humour* (Defenestration) *to horror* (Murky Depths)*, mystery* (FMAM) *to mainstream* (Underground Voices)*, and everything in between. His work also appears in several paperback anthologies, including the Read by Dawn series, The One That Got Away, and Damnation & Dames. You can follow him at* www.briangrantross.com

Noir People

Bruce Boston

If noir people were the world
we would forever roam
the crooked nighttime streets
and brutal alleys of a city
of shifting shadows,
our own shadows
rippling across sidewalks
and the dim facades
of deserted buildings,
swelling and shrinking
behind us and before us
as we moved from one
lamppost to the next.

If noir people were the world
color would abandon us
to be superceded by
a range of shadow shades
in subtle gray distinctions,
by stark chiaroscuro contrasts
invisible to a world of color.

We would live in cheap
hotels or tenement flats,
drink our liquor straight up,
tell world-weary jokes
and crack cynical smiles
from the sides of our mouths.

If noir people were the world
death could come swiftly
and without reprieve,
-- the fast flare of a bullet,
the moonlight flash
of a knife driven home --
and our blood spilled
upon the damp pavement
would be no more
than the color of night.

Bruce Boston *is the author of more than fifty books and chapbooks, including the novels* The Guardener's Tale *and* Stained Glass Rain. *His writing has received the Bram Stoker Award, a Pushcart Prize, the Asimov's Readers Award, and the Grand Master Award of the Science Fiction Poetry Association.*

THE EQUILIBRIUM OF LUCK

Teresa Hawk

The fire door slammed behind me, and then I saw it. Far away, at the other end of the hall, a blurry, crawly thing moved out of the shadows. I took a few steps forward and refocused. The creature moved like an oversized, mutant dog. *Is that a werewolf?* My brain rejected such a ridiculous idea and concentrated on the color of the thing. *That's pale, human flesh, not fur,* I reassured myself, while approaching in a cautious fighting stance. *Damn, I wish I had a gun right now.* The creature skulked on all fours towards me. I stopped dead. Its hairy, undulating head hung low, like a bull ready to charge. Then I pushed the button on my collar microphone.

"Officer Moore to Control," I said into my radio, inching closer.

"Go ahead, Moore," Dispatch said.

"There's something here. I've got a naked guy. Crawling. Like a dog! He's coming right for me. He looks like he's four-oh-eight, or maybe he's four-twenty-one."

"What's your twenty, Dawn?"

I wished there were surveillance cameras in the hotel so they could see this. "I'm on the ninth floor."

"Gonzalez, go to the ninth floor of the Sky Tower," Dispatch said.

"Copy," Gonzalez said.

"Something's wrong with this guy," I said into the radio as I sprinted towards him a few yards before stopping myself again at a safe distance. Surveying the scene, I considered a scenario where naked-dog-man was the diversion, and his partner jumped me to do God-knows-what.

The man wobbled and struggled to crawl towards me. Unable to lift his head, he whimpered like a wounded animal. Something about his feeble plea eased my paranoia.

"He's not drunk. He's definitely injured. Four-twenty-one," I reported into the radio.

"Do you want us to call paramedics?"

"Uh, Yeah," I said with too much attitude, then I corrected myself, "Affirmative. He's very sick. We need paramedics."

"Copy. Gonzalez, grab the AED bag," Dispatch said.

"I've already got it," he said, "I'm on the elevator now."

"Bike Two, go to the Sky Garage for paramedic escort." Dispatch said.

"Copy," Bike Two replied.

"Are you okay?" I asked the man.

He could not respond. The nude guest teetered back and forth, struggling to support his own weight. I stood next to him, careful to maintain my closed stance. His head hung so low that it dragged on the carpet. His skin was pale. I scanned him for bruises, cuts, or blood, but found nothing.

"Can you hear me?"

He said nothing.

"Moore, Can you give us a description of the man," Dispatch asked in my earpiece.

"White. Male. Adult. Naked. Conscious, but he can't talk."

"How old is he?"

"I can't see his face." Judging from his middle-aged spread and the gray of his faded hair, I guessed, "I don't know, maybe fifty."

"Copy. Ask him his name."

"What's your name?" I snapped on my latex gloves. The sick man whimpered again before collapsing on the floor. I bent down and touched his shoulder. "Stay with me, buddy. Just breathe."

The half-moons of his fingernails turned blue. His skin was cold and clammy, his breathing shallow. Helpless, I watched him slip into shock.

"One-one to Control, I'm on my way," Jackson said.

"Copy," Dispatch said.

"He's breathing, but no longer responsive," I reported on the radio.

Gonzalez ran out of the elevator and dropped the AED bag on the ground beside me. He unzipped it. The naked man seized.

"Shit!" I was hoping that wouldn't happen. Then a mother exited the elevator with her daughter and headed towards us. I stood up and blocked their path holding my arms out wide. "Wait here. You don't want to see this."

The mom nodded and pulled her daughter close. Then I dashed into the linen room and startled a sleeping housekeeper. The old Latino woman jumped up and acted like she was working.

"Do you have any sheets?" I asked.

"What?"

"Sheets! I need a sheet."

"I was just—" The housekeeper fumbled.

"I don't care. I'm not here to bust you." I yanked three bath towels off her cart and ran out of the room. I dashed past the mother and daughter towards the limp, sick man on the floor. Then I draped two skimpy, budget-hotel towels over his crotch and placed a folded one under his head.

"He's still breathing, but I'm ready," Gonzalez said as he inserted the prongs of an oxygen tube into the man's nostrils.

"You can pass now," I said to the mother, who then carried her daughter around us. They disappeared down the hall and into their room. Officer Jackson and a Bike Unit stepped off the elevator to join the growing circle of officers around the sick guest.

"Where did he come from?" Jackson asked.

"I don't know. I opened that door," I pointed left, "and found him crawling from the opposite end of the hall." I pointed right.

"Go see if any of those doors are ajar," Jackson ordered the Bike Officer while gesturing in the same direction as me. Jackson bent down and said, "What's your name?"

The man did not respond. Another officer escorted a couple paramedics off the next elevator. Their gurney couldn't fit through the crowded hallway.

"Everyone step back," Jackson ordered, letting the paramedics through.

I noted the time in my memo pad.

"What's his name," the paramedic asked while clamping a pulse oximeter onto her patient's fingertip.

"We don't know. He can't talk," I said.

The paramedics took the man's vitals and injected him with a clear liquid.

"What's your name," the paramedic asked.

I watched the digital numbers on the device increase and thought that must be a good sign. The man tried to speak, but nothing audible came out.

"What's you're name," she repeated.

"Matt Oleman," the man mumbled.

I wrote his name into my memo pad.

"Matt, do you have any medical conditions we should know about?"

"M-meth. I used to be a meth addict."

"Did you take any meth today, Matt?" The other paramedic asked.

"N-no."

"Did you take *any* drugs today," he asked.

"No. I'm clean."

Jackson rolled her eyes, "Yeah, right," she said under her breath to me. "Moore, call Dispatch and see what room Matthew Oleman is registered in."

"Okay." I went into the linen room and dialed Dispatch from a house phone.

"How's it going up there?" The dispatcher's calming voice sounded, deep, smooth and clear, like a nighttime DJ on a soul station. Even though I had worked at this Vegas property for over a year, I had never met the man behind the voice and had no idea what he looked like.

"Paramedics arrived at sixteen thirty-six," I read from my notes.

"Got it. Do you have a name yet?"

"Yes. Matthew Oleman."

"How's that spelled?"

"Oscar, Lima, Echo, Mike, Alpha, November—I think."

"Hold on. I'm checking," he said. The sound of fast clicking keys followed. The housekeeper made a concerned face.

"Is he sick?"

"Yes. Just stay in here," I said and turned away. "Whatcha got for me?"

"Nothing yet. No one with that name is registered here. Maybe he checked out yesterday. I'll do some digging," he said, tapping on the keyboard. "This might take awhile. I'll call you if I find anything."

"Okay, bye." I said before hanging up the phone.

When I returned to the scene, paramedics were rolling the patient away on the gurney. Mr. Oleman shook and jerked so violently that he kicked off his sheet and almost tumbled off the stretcher. Somehow, the paramedics managed to keep him from falling.

"It hurts so bad." Matt groaned as he pushed hard against the thin mattress.

"Matt, calm down," the paramedic said as she strapped him down with restraints.

"Oh MY God! It hurts!"

"Relax, Matt," The other paramedic said as they rolled him into the elevator. When the doors slid closed, Jackson looked at me.

"Dispatch couldn't find his room. They're still searching," I said.

"All the doors on this floor were closed," Jackson said. "Go search the stairwell." She looked at her watch. "Everyone else, back to your posts."

Straggling officers migrated towards the bay of elevators.

"Call me in the office, if you find anything," Jackson said while pushing the down arrow. "I'll go try to track this guy down in the system."

After everyone left, I stepped into the linen room. I took a disposable cup from a cart and removed its thin, plastic wrapper, then poured water from the utility sink and went to the hall to add some ice. I took a deep breath, drank half, and took the rest along. After entering the east stairwell, I headed downward. Looking for bare footprints on the dusty metal steps made sense to me, but I found nothing. After clearing a few flights, I realized that I should have gone upward instead. Matt would have been too weak to climb stairs. He would have come from above. But before I could turn around, the stairwell started to rumble and quake and it triggered a memory. "No way," I said aloud as I dropped my cup and galloped down the stairs.

And there he was, ass end up with his junk swinging free. Matt crawled like a dog down the stairs right in front of me.

"Matt! Stop!"

He ignored me as he crept towards a dwarf-sized, sea foam green door of the fifth floor landing.

"No! Matt, don't." I grabbed the handrail as the ground shook more violently.

As I plodded down the stairs behind him, naked Matt crawled through the locked door. His ghost feet dragged across the threshold and then disappeared from sight. I rattled the door lock. Jagged lines of bright light radiated through cracks from the other side, then dimmed to a soft glow before going black. Then the tremors stopped. I smelled a hint of grapefruit. Feeling confused and defeated, I fell to my knees. Then I swore I could hear the rolling, happy sound of spinning slot machine wheels. The congratulatory progression of three chimes climbed their scale just like the last time. And when I heard the festive bells and the sound of fake coins dropping, I punched the door. A lucky someone in the casino just hit the jackpot.

A few hours later, I sat in the stubby, hotel hand-me-down armchair in my boss's office. I had given up on comfort. The best I hoped for was to maintain a professional posture in the chair. Supervisor Wright's lofty position behind his heavy walnut desk, forced me to look up at him from my low seat. I shuffled around before settling on the edge and leaning forward. *What an awful chair.* From the corner, Jackson's squeaky, office chair groaned as she stretched behind her much smaller, rickety, metal desk.

"We called you in to debrief you regarding your four-21 earlier," Supervisor Wright said. "The name of the injured guest you found was Matthew Goldman. He went into cardiac arrest on the elevator and died in the ambulance before it departed the property."

The news did not surprise me, but it still stung.

Wright studied my response. "Our detectives found his room on the tenth floor. No drugs or paraphernalia were in the room." Wright said. He took a long pause and slowed his pace. "We are waiting for the Coroner's Report, but evidence suggests that Mr. Goldman hemorrhaged and died from internal bleeding. His mattress and clothing were soaked in blood. It looked like he got undressed, took a shower, and then panicked. He must have went into the hall looking for help. Then he stumbled down a flight of stairs to where you found him on the ninth."

So, I did hear something up there, I thought to myself. Jackson raised an eyebrow. Wright read my face.

"There was nothing you could have done to save him," Wright said.

My expression went blank while I reprocessed the incident with this new information. *I could have found him sooner, if we weren't goofing off.*

Jackson rolled her chair forward. *Screech, screech, squawk.*

"Did you hear me Dawn? It's not your fault he died. He bled to death," Wright said.

"Okay."

"We have counseling services available through Human Resources if you need to talk—"

"I'm fine. It was awful to watch him suffer, but I'll be fine." The threat of tears pressed me to end the conversation. I refused to cry at work, especially in front of my boss.

Wright sensed my discomfort.

"All right. We're here if you need to talk," he said.

"May I go?"

"You're dismissed." Wright pretended to type.

Calmly, I left the office and stepped into the alley. The early morning sun warmed my face. I sat on the bench under a sign that read

Designated Employee Smoking Area and pulled a long, brown cigarette out of my pocket, lit it with a match, and inhaled. I had bummed this one off a porter named Etienne. He had always been so nice to me, and I didn't even know his last name. Not too long ago, I discovered that smoking made the stale air inside the casino tolerable. It also delivered a delightful, tingly buzz. I had never smoked before this job, but more and more, I found myself bumming cigs. But I refused to buy a pack of my own. That would make me a *real* smoker.

I stared at the burning cherry of my exotic cigarette. The purple of my bruised knuckles matched the shiny, twin band around the filter. *Stupid*. I had never punched a door before. I knew better. If I hadn't been wearing latex gloves, my knuckles would have split wide open. Controlling my anger got harder each passing night. It bothered me, but no one else cared. Anger was the only acceptable emotion to express in such a macho job. We all had to be tough.

A man in a reflective yellow shirt came riding around the corner on a mountain bike. It was Gonzalez. He rode up to me. "Miss Moore, where you at for the rest of the night?"

"Heading back to the tower after I get back from lunch," I said, blowing smoke. "That naked guy died."

"Yeah, I heard. I'm on bikes for the second half of my double."

"I *knew* I heard something up on ten. How long were we up there? What if they find out?"

"They won't."

"If it weren't for our stupid, little bitchfest, I would've found him sooner. We coulda saved him."

"Or, you might have been making rounds so fast that you missed him," he said.

"I guess." I looked away as tears pushed from inside again.

"Don't worry about it. We did all we could."

"I wish we carried guns inside." I pointed at the pistol on his hip, and then took a final drag before changing the topic. "Hey, by the way, did someone hit a jackpot tonight?"

"Huh? Oh, yeah. Some old broad won two hundred grand on the Wiz Oz progressive slots by the perfume store. Why?"

"What time?"

"Sarah didn't say. Why?" Gonzalez tapped away on his shiny new iPhone with both thumbs.

"Just curious," I said, crushing the cigarette butt with my melee boot.

His phone chimed twice, and he read a new text message, "Sarah says right before she went to lunch." He paused, "that was a quarter to five."

"The same time naked guy died," I pointed out.

"No shit? Well, that's a helluva coincidence."

Three weeks later, I watched a parade of drunks from my linen room window-perch on the top of the Sky Tower. From thirty-five stories high, they looked like retarded, stampeding rats scurrying away from floodwaters. When the horde got to the Boulevard, they all stopped to ogle the night sky. Most of them managed to stay out of traffic while they waited for the fourth of July fireworks to begin. *Good for them.* With the swift determination of a predator, I took the service elevator down to the sixth floor, hiked to the east stairwell, dashed down the steps, and knelt before the mysterious, tiny, access door.

As I snatched a pouch from my uniform's breast pocket, I remembered how my belittling ex-husband had tried to teach me how to pick a lock many years ago. In his typical impatient anger, he shoved me out of the way and did it himself. So, it had felt wonderful to liberate this particular set of lock-picks from his car a week before I left him. I never really thought I'd use them, but for a more gentle refresher course, I found a "How To Pick a Deadbolt Lock" video on You-Tube. Ever since I saw Matt crawl through this weird, little, locked door, I had been practicing on a deadbolt that I bought at Home Depot for twenty-nine dollars and ninty-seven cents.

There was no doorknob, just the lock. So, I inserted the tension wrench so that it pointed away from the bolt, and then raked inside the top of the lock three times. Wiggling the short hook inside the key-hole, I felt each pin slide into the shoe-line one by one until it released. *Excellent.* Then I twisted the tension wrench clockwise towards the hinges and felt the bolt slide open. A little pressure popped the small door wide open.

As I peeked through the miniature doorway for the first time, the stale scent of thick dust, motor oil, old grapefruit, and decay accosted my nostrils. Out of reflex, I gagged and covered my mouth. The darkness of the room made it impossible to gauge its size. A small shaft of light leaking between the doorway and my body reflected off something within arm's reach. Stretching upward into the darkness, I felt the cruddy surface of a bare light bulb. Blindly, I grasped at the air until I snagged a dirty string with a heavy, rusty washer tied to the end. I yanked harder than necessary and the dim bulb lit.

I crouched through the doorway and duck-walked into the room. The low ceiling made it impossible for me to stand, and I avoided crawling, because broken glass covered the dirty floor. The carpet felt squishy, like wet, matted, moldy shag. A cot mattress laid flat on the floor, shoved up against the wall. I plopped down on the lumpy wad and wrestled my Maglite out of its snapped case on my utility belt. As I swept a beam of light into the shadows of the room, I saw a thick blanket of dusty spider webs covering a barrier of broken furniture.

The silence in the room was eerie. My radio traffic had gone quiet. No reception. There were about a dozen dead zones in the hotel and casino, and it looked like I just found another one. But aside from the lack of officer chatter, the silence was more profound—more than still-ness. It was total absence. No white noise. The sound of my own breathing seemed to be absorbed by the acoustical anomaly of the room.

I wanted to see what hid behind the stacks of broken junk and old cobwebs, but I didn't want to touch any of it. For all my public bravado, I had a phobia of spiders, of all bugs really, and of worms, and all other creepy crawlies. As I scuttled across the floor, my knees screamed at me in pain, so I kneeled by the closest stack of trashed furniture. I sucked on the flashlight handle and pulled a splintered chair leg from the pile. Using it to swipe away a dried tangle of webs, it became clear to me that some sort of image was painted on the con-crete block wall.

My careful progress was slow and I failed to keep spider webs from touching my skin. Somehow I managed to suppress my squeamish re-pulsion as I yanked on pieces of broken furniture and threw them be-hind me. Soon, I was thrashing away at the barrier with wild abandon. Then suddenly, from a space between a broken table lamp and a dresser drawer, a pair of eyes flashed back at me. I gasped, dropping the flashlight out of my mouth, and lurching backwards as best a per-son working on her knees could. When I pointed the light back into the dark crevasse where I saw the human eyes, I discovered they were part of a macabre portrait.

Diving back into the pile, I revealed more and more of the mural. Faces of all ages and races looked back at me with expressions of hor-ror. Men and women appeared to be either frightened, or in pain, or both. As I examined the images, I found Matthew Goldman among them. I knew his face well, because it had haunted me in my sleep for weeks after his death. And now he was here, last in line, frozen on the wall with the others.

The others... I shuddered at what that might mean. Underneath his face, the date of his death, June 13, 2012 was printed in the neatest of typefaces. And under that, over a blank patch of concrete, was more print that read: **Betty Travers: $197,874**. I dug frantically. The mural stretched off to the left around the room. To the right, the wall was blank, as if it was a page of history yet to be written.

I exposed dozens and dozens of faces. Each had a date, name, and dollar amount underneath. As I looked to the left, the jackpots got smaller and the images looked older. *Reverse inflation.* I traced my finger over Matthew's portrait. It didn't feel like any paint I'd ever touched before. The images seemed to be burned onto the surface of the concrete, but in vivid (almost projected) color. They faded just the slightest bit along with the historical hairstyles and eyewear of past decades.

A portrait of a woman with one of those big, frizzy eighties hairdos caught my attention. I stopped to consider her, because she wore her hair the way I had way back in junior high school. Under her head, the date (which I assumed was her date of death) was November 14, 1989. And then I noticed the name and corresponding jackpot printed clearly under the young woman's face:

Matthew Goldman: $87,809.

Teresa Hawk *lives in a "classified" location somewhere in the Nevada desert where she weaves an endless parade of colorful characters into macabre tales that keep readers up all night. Her earliest influences include; Stephen King, Clive Barker, Wes Craven, and Edgar Allan Poe. At age twelve, she wrote her first supernatural horror story on wide-ruled notebook paper with a No. 2 pencil. As it circulated, she found the horrified reactions of teachers combined with the squealing delight of her peers to be powerfully addicting. She's been writing ever since. Over the course of her career, she has been a technical writer, published academic, and copy editor. Now, building on those literary skills, she injects her dark humor and twisted imagination of the weird, surreal, and grotesque into gritty, character-driven horror. Prepare to have your perception altered, and hold on, because it's going to be a wild ride into the darkness!*

CTHULHU'S CAMPAIGN SONG

Robert Laughlin

(to the tune of "Columbia, the Gem of the Ocean"; 12 lines)

Election Day is once more upon us.
Demands on a leader are great.
Voters once again have the onus
Of choosing the next chief of state.

There's a new face that merits your attention;
Granted good looks are not his forte.
No, his scales mustn't cause you apprehension.
Cast your vote for Cthulhu today!

Cast your vote for Cthulhu today!
And his program will sweep you away!
Take this great nation to the next dimension!
Cast your vote for Cthulhu today!

Robert Laughlin *lives in Chico, California. He is the founder of the Micro Award for flash fiction, and has published eighty flash stories of his own. His website is at www.pw.org/content/robert_laughlin.*

Gothic Window

Richard H. Fay

Through the stone-traced panes I see
The ancestral plot below.
A pale murky mist obscures
The white marble monuments
That mark the graves of my kin.
Time has worn the names and dates
But cannot erase the past.

In the foggy gloom I see
Ghostly figures beckoning.
Restless spirits summon me
To join their ghastly legions.
Empty skulls stare eagerly.
Frightened by the dreadful scene
I swiftly avert my gaze.

Mirrored in the glass I see
A darkly shrouded shadow;
The reaper stands behind me.
Death's cold voice whispers my name.
I feel his frigid touch
Upon my shoulder.
The window shatters.

☙✠❧

Richard H. Fay *currently resides in upstate New York with his wife and two cats. Formerly a laboratory technician-turned-home educator, Richard now spends his days juggling numerous writing and art projects. History, myth, folklore, and legend serve as inspiration for his creative endeavours. Many of the fruits of his labour have appeared in various e-zines, print magazines, and anthologies.*

The Flute of the Dead

Jack Campbell, Jr.

Len's breath filled the flute with life as his fingers danced over its hollow reed body. The kiva's thick coffin of stucco walls resonated with a solemn song for the dead, and those soon to join them. The Eaters approached. Neither Len, nor his people, could stop them. This world was ending. The time for migration approached. Survivors fled toward the great cliff dwellings, hoping for salvation.

Len played for the Spider Woman, who led his people to this place, the intersection of the great roads. She would lead them to their new world, one free of the terrible nightmare of the Eaters.

Len finished the song. His senses returned. The fire baked his skin. Screams and war cries invaded the space vacated by the song. The rich, earthen scent of the kiva filled his nose. Len's brother Honovi climbed down the ladder from the roof hatch. Blood and sweat coated his lean, muscular body.

"What are you doing?" Honovi said. He kicked dirt over the fire, smothering it. "You are going to lead the Eaters to you and give them a fire to roast you."

"We won't be here much longer."

"I agree. While you play your flute, people die."

"I played a song for their deaths."

"You will be playing for your own if we don't leave."

"We have to wait for the other clans."

"They are dead, Len."

The clans spread from the canyon's center like the rays from the sun, but the farther they travelled from the light, the darker the shadows they discovered. Their father Shuman's recent death had been an omen of destruction. The responsibility for their people's survival fell to Honovi.

"Put that thing away," Honovi said, handing Len a bow and quiver of arrows.

Len rubbed his thumb along the flute's worn body, feeling its imperfections. Len slid his flute into the quiver, resting it within the forest of reed shafts. Honovi helped him up. Len's legs trembled numbly. Feeling returned as blood rushed to his feet.

Len and Honovi climbed the ladder onto the kiva roof. Stars flickered in an otherwise black night. The Eaters, friends of the darkness, timed their attack to coincide with the new moon. Fires lit paths between the kivas, leading Len's people through the quickest route. Len had expected to see great numbers of his people in the paths. They lay empty.

"Where is everyone else?"

"Dead or dying," Honovi said. "I couldn't save our village."

"We must follow the Spider Woman to the fourth world," Len said.

"I did't want to leave." Honovi pointed to the dwellings built into the face of the cliff. "Look at what we made. You want to leave it and start over?"

"No. The gods do."

Len retrieved the ladder and lowered it over the side of the kiva. He followed Honovi down to the path.

"The gods didn't cause this. We did." Honovi strung an arrow into his bow. "If the southern clans hadn't gone into their lands, the Eaters wouldn't have followed the roads back to the canyon. We should have stayed here."

"That isn't what our people do."

"We should learn," Honovi said. "We will take the north road."

"What about everyone else?"

"No one is coming."

Len and Honovi moved through the lit path toward the north road. Horrific cries bounced off the canyon walls. The Eaters howled with each kill. It was their world, now.

"How could you possibly think we could fight the Eaters?" Len asked. "They have warriors. We have farmers and craftsmen."

"Then we should bash their skulls with our clay pots. Better than being slaughtered like animals. I will not lie down and be dinner."

"They believe eating a man gains you his strength and wisdom," Len said.

"Then I can't wait to see their disappointment when they meet you."

"Quiet." Len heard footsteps. He smelled blood. Len led his brother around the corner of a kiva, sliding along the wall. His heart pounded. Blood raced through his body. His muscles tensed.

Len peeked around the cover of the wall to see an Eater. Strange painted designs covered its muscular body and pale face. It moved through shadows, avoiding the fires' harsh light. In one hand, The Eater carried a chipped rock axe. In the other, a woman's severed arm. The Eater licked its saliva-drenched lips and bit into the forearm. Sinew and tendon snapped as muscle separated from bone. Blood trickled over its decorated jaw.

Honovi shoved Len aside and raised his bow. His arrow found a home in the Eater's pale throat. The Eater collapsed, gurgling blood. Honovi picked up the axe and smashed the Eater's skull. Gore splattered Honovi's face. He looked at Len through a mask of blood and brain.

"We could have slipped by," Len said.

"That is my enemy," Honovi said, pointing at the painted corpse. "I will kill as many as I can find." Honovi offered the axe to Len.

"There's blood on it," Len said, shaking his head.

"Then we know it is a good axe."

Honovi lashed the axe to his quiver and walked away. Len gazed upon the Eater's lifeless body. His flute beckoned him play a song to escort the Eater's soul to the deadlands. He knew that Honovi would never allow it. Len quietly hummed a short section of the song of the dead. The beautiful, tragic melody vibrated on his lips. It was all he could do.

Len caught up with Honovi at the edge of the north road. Bodies littered the path, Dead Eaters scattered among families. Even the enemy had been eaten. The monsters consumed their own dead.

"An Eater will die for every one of my people. I swear to it." Honovi said, flexing his hands around his bow. They begged for blood. Len reached out to touch his shoulder. Honovi shrugged him off and walked up the road.

Len followed his brother, humming the song of the dead. Here lay the legless body of Kachina. Once a great dancer, the Eaters had harvested her body for its richest meat. Len hummed for her. There lay the flesh-stripped corpse of Catori, recognizable only by his massive hands. Len's tune was for him, as well. They stepped over Sihu, the beautiful bowl-maker whom Honovi had been arranged to marry. She lay naked, raped, and slain. Len's heart swelled with song. He sang. Honovi turned and snatched him by the shoulders.

"Quiet! What do think you are doing?" Honovi said, his eyes wet.

"I was just — "

"Do you want every Eater in this place to come down upon us?" Honovi shook his brother. "They are dead."

"I'm sorry."

Honovi's hands trembled. "Just stop. Please. Stop."

Len embraced his brother. Warm tears wet his shoulder. Honovi turned away and wiped his eyes on his forearm.

"Keep moving and stay silent," Honovi said.

"You couldn't have stopped them," Len said.

"It was my duty to try."

Len and Honovi travelled north. Honovi walked slumped, crushed under the weight of his responsibility. They passed many bodies, some familiar, some not. Women had been tortured; children slaughtered where they stood. Len barely recognized the dead Eaters, except for their painted skin. Death rendered them human.

"My people are gone," Honovi whispered. "I failed them."

"You make them proud," Len said.

"Do I make you proud? A chief weeping at the sight of the dead?"

"I am proud of a brother's courage to grieve."

Honovi looked up to the stars. "Our father would have found a way to save his people."

"All happens as the Spider Woman planned," Len said. "Nothing we do can prevent the destruction of this world, any more than the Eaters can stop our migration to the next."

"How do you not get sick of those stories?"

"No one should be sickened by the truth."

"So many died."

"They will be remembered in songs."

"Songs are your strength, not mine," Honovi said.

"All hearts sing. Open yours and love for your people will pour from it like water from a bowl."

Eater corpses became commonplace. Honovi's mood elevated with each one they passed. Len felt relentless dread. Warriors had recently fought a battle here.

Len heard a low moan. He held up his hand, signaling Honovi to stay silent. They crept low, approaching a wounded Eater. It aspirated blood. An arrow had pierced the Eater's chest, deflating its left lung. It spoke quietly. The sounds were familiar, the tone like a prayer, but the words incomprehensible. Honovi stood above the Eater and drew back his bow. The foreign words came louder and faster. Honovi drove an arrow through the Eater's right eye, silencing him forever.

Guilt flooded into Len. Honovi had executed a defenseless, dying man. Len's eyes betrayed his thoughts.

"I need a warrior, not a shaman," Honovi said. "This thing was an animal, and I killed him like one. You carry arrows along with that flute. I pray you know how to use them."

Len imagined his executed enemy's family anticipating their father's return, as he had waited for Shuman's. How long would hope persist? Friend and foe changed with perspective. The enemy at his feet had likely embraced another as brother. A nearby war cry broke Len's urge to play for the Eater.

"Come on," Len said, already running. The shouts of battle grew louder as they dashed through the darkness.

The hunter Cha'Tima brawled with three Eaters. Len tackled the first one he reached. They rolled in a tangled mess upon the road. The Eater came to rest on top of Len, strangling him with thick, leathery hands. Len clawed at the Eater's face. The stars faded. The hands relaxed suddenly. Len coughed, choking on the Eater's blood. A shaft ran through its painted chest. Cha'Tima lifted Len to his feet.

"That was my last arrow," Cha'Tima said.

"Here, take mine," Len said. "You will have more use for them than I."

"Many thanks."

Len removed his flute before exchanging quivers with Cha'Tima and slung the instrument across his back.

Honovi fought two Eaters, his bow in one hand and the seized Eater axe in the other. Len swung his empty bow like a club, striking an Eater in the back. It turned to face Len with a nerve-shattering roar, falling silent as Honovi split his skull. Len's arrow flew from Cha'Tima's bow and drove through the remaining Eater's heart.

"My Chief," Cha'Tima said. "I feared I was alone."

"As did we," Honovi said. "Together we can give Len many songs to sing."

"I hear them," Len said. "They come in packs."

Len searched the shadows for movement. Silhouettes approached from the north, carrying rock knives and axes. The tree line to the east rustled. Eaters crept out of the foliage. The low speech of the Eaters slipped to his ears from the south.

"Get out of here, Len," Honovi said.

"No."

"You don't have any arrows. You couldn't fight when you did. Leave."

"No, I'm not abandoning you."

"Cha'Tima, are you prepared to die?"

"I am, my Chief."

"Len will sing songs for us. He will carry us to the deadlands on his flute."

"Come with me," Len said.

"If we all run, we all die," Honovi said. "Go. Find your Spider Woman."

Honovi shouted a war cry and charged at the Eaters to the north. Cha'Tima drew his bow and fired arrows at the Eaters who emerged from the eastern tree line.

"Listen to your Chief," Cha'Tima said. "Go!"

Len ran west, tears filling his eyes. Cha-Tima fell under a flood of axes. Eaters surrounded Honovi. He shot an arrow into an enemy point blank. He snapped off the head in the screaming Eater's chest and shoved the splintered shaft into its throat. A spray of warm blood painted Honovi's face.

The Eaters jumped upon him. Two hung off his back, biting his shoulder meat. Honovi fought, crippling Eaters with brute strength. He tore an axe from an Eater's grip, and then buried it in another's skull. More went low, tearing at Honovi's succulent calves. Honovi wailed as Eaters piled upon him.

Len ran west, deep into the forest. The dark engulfed him. He slowed to listen. His panting breath broke the unnerving silence of the forest. Death muted the constant cadence of life. He heard the low growl of an Eater stalking him through the trees. Len moved as quickly and silently as possible. Still, the growl grew. The Eater could see in the dark and was an expert hunter. The growl was close. Len ran.

Len did not see the ravine until he stumbled into it, twisting his ankle as he fell into a ragged crevice. A distinct rattle silenced his cry of pain. His fall awakened a sleeping rattlesnake. Len crawled away from the sound.

"Brother Snake, I am Len. Perhaps you knew my father, Chief Shuman. On a warm night, when he was a young man, you slithered into his chamber. There, you found him, along with his young wife, pregnant with my brother, the great Chief Honovi. He spoke to you, asking for your blessing of strength upon his unborn son. He begged you to spare their lives. I'm not my father. I'm only a musician. But if you spare my life as you did theirs, I will play you a song on my flute."

The Eater approached the ravine. He looked down curiously upon Len, who still sat on the ground. The Eater moved prepared to attack.

Len removed his flute from the quiver. The Eater took a defensive step back, and then laughed when he saw what Len held. Len drew a deep breath and brought the reed flute to his lips.

Len played a song of his life. He played a melody of birth, of grow-ing up in the shadow of Shuman, and then of his brother. He played for those who had died, that they would not be forgotten. He played for those who survived, that they would find the Spider Woman. Len freed his spirit through the flute. The tune consumed him. He saw it; breathed it. It lingered in the air, caressing his soul. He soaked in the warmth of the music and waited for death.

The Eater dropped down into the ravine, its mouth whetted. The Eater grinned as it stalked its prey. It did not see the snake until it had already struck. Fangs sank deep into The Eater's leg, pumping venom into muscle. The Eater screamed. It tore off the hissing snake and hurled it aside. Blood drained slowly from twin punctures in The Eater's calf. The Eater ran away into forest, crying in his strange, but familiar language.

Len opened his eyes. "Thank you, Brother Snake," Len said, sliding his flute back into the quiver. "You have blessed my family." Len pulled himself to his feet and limped west on a swollen ankle.

Len walked for many days, past the edge of the forest and through the desert, following the sun's path. He could not find food or water. The heat baked Len's skin, yet he was thankful for the sun. Darkness brought dreams of loved ones' chewed corpses. Every desert sound seemed to herald an Eater's approach. Len spent many restless nights watching the new moon grow full.

On a late summer afternoon, Len reached a great canyon. He could go no farther. He found a small tree and sat in its shade. Len removed his flute from the quiver and played the death song for himself. His fingers ached as they faltered over the reed body. His brain felt slug-gish, forgetting notes. His breath struggled to pass through his dry mouth. The flute wept. It mourned for Len, begging for his safe pas-sage to the deadlands, where he would find his family again.

A figure approached from the horizon, the Spider Woman, shim-mering in radiant heat, coming to take Len to the fourth world. Len hoped his song would please her, as weary as it sounded. His weak melody called his people to gather in the great canyon, where they would start again.

Len played his flute until his breathing ceased, and the music died.

When he's not stepping on his son's Legos, **Jack Campbell, Jr.** *writes dark fiction in Lawrence, KS. His writing has appeared in several venues, including* **Dark Eclipse, Hungur Magazine,** *and* **Insomnia Press.** *He is a contributor to* **The Confabulator Cafe.** *You can learn more about Jack and his writing at www.jackcampbelljr.com.*

SKINJACKING

Sarina Dorie

After dropping candy into each Trick-or-treater's bucket, Dolores watched the gaggle of children run off to the next house. Two children dressed as pirates remained. Neither had buckets. They simply stood there, staring up at her with bright, blue eyes. Dolores stepped forward onto the front step.

"I like her skin," said the little girl.

The little boy shrugged. "Yeah, it's interesting."

Dolores touched her weathered face, wondering if this little girl could be serious. She certainly seemed earnest. Was this child saying she thought she was still pretty, even at her ripe old age? Wasn't that sweet.

"I haven't ever had wrinkles before," the little girl said.

"Aren't you just charming!" Dolores laughed, handing them each a piece of candy which they stared at, heads tilted to the sides. "Of course you haven't any wrinkles now, but someday you will get them."

"I really would like wrinkles now," said the girl. "Would you trade me?"

Confused, Dolores held up a mini Kit-Kat. "Do you want a different kind of chocolate?"

The girl sighed in exasperation. "Would you trade me skins?"

Dolores eyed the cute, little girl in her pirate costume, blond curls bounding. Her skin was smooth and flawless as porcelain. Oh, to be young again. . . . Dolores shook her head. "You have no idea what I would give to be your age again."

"Perfect!" The little girl smiled, her grin stretching across her cheeks, growing wider until it reached her ears, every pearl-like tooth exposed in that monstrous grin. Dolores watched in frozen horror as the girl grabbed her upper lip and peeled her face back like it was nothing more than a hood. The child slipped the skin and clothes off in one heap, revealing a bloody lump of a body. Pulsing veins covered sinewy muscle. Glistening globs of fat clung in clusters around pumping organs.

Dolores stood rooted to the spot, unblinking and scarcely able to breath. Only now did she regain herself enough to back toward her door. The boy picked up the human hide from the ground, holding it out.

The little girl looked to Dolores with the same blue eyes as before. "Okay, now it's your turn. . . ."

As a child, **Sarina Dorie** *dreamed of being an astronaut/archeologist/fashion designer/illustrator/writer. After years of dedication and hard work, most of Sarina's dreams have come true; in addition to teaching art, she is a writer/artist/fashion designer/ belly dancer. She has taught English overseas South Korea and in the JET program in Japan, and worked as a copy editor. She has shown her art internationally and sold illustrations to magazines. Sarina's soon to be published novel,* **Silent Moon,** *won second place in the* **Duel on the Delta Contest,** *second place in the* **Golden Rose,** *third place in the* **Winter Rose Contest** *and third in the* **Ignite the Flame Contest.** *Her unpublished novel,* **Wrath of the Tooth Fairy** *won first place in the* **Golden Claddagh** *and in the* **Golden Rose** *contests. She has sold short stories to over thirty magazines and anthologies including* **Daily Science Fiction, Cosmos, Penumbra, Perihelion, Bards and Sages, Neo-Opsis, Flagship, Allasso, New Myths, Untied Shoelaces of the Mind,** *and* **Crossed Genres** *to name a few.*

Now, if only Jack Sparrow asks her to marry him, all her dreams will come true. www.sarinadorie.com

Love's Cadaver

WC Roberts

Love's cadaver in your arms
was flayed alive, now it speaks

remembering your first encounter
in a sidewalk cafe, on the streets of Prague

where you once played soldier
steeped in the Red Death, a pawn of Moscow

and East Berlin. What gives? The alms
leave a grotto in your ribcage

where love's melancholy bird used to sing
madrigals and old plainsong favorites

to amuse your comrades
and their hired, sylphlike Czechs

drowned in ambergris and Meershaum
-- full-bodied, bottom-fermented --

before the armored drive to Vienna,
opening death's gate to war

by rad, gas-masked Carnival attrition
in shrouds of fog and catacombs

here, beneath the Stephansdom,
where the hardest fighting goes on

in our letters home, the false
and reassuring words *of anonymity.*

WC Roberts *lives in a mobile home up on Bixby Hill, on land that was once the county dump. The only window looks out on a ragged scarecrow standing in a field of straw and dressed in WC's own discarded clothes. WC dreams of the desert, of finally getting his first television set, and of ravens. Above all, he writes, and has had poems published in* Strange Horizons, Apex, Space & Time Magazine, Mindflights, Aoife's Kiss, Big Pulp, Star*Line, *and others.*

Seeing Red

Michelle Ann King

Halden's mother called out his name, but he ignored her and slammed out of the house. He felt bad about upsetting her, but he just couldn't go along with it any more. Ever since they'd left Earth, she'd been obsessed with these pointless, irrelevant rituals.

She called them celebrations, but what did anyone have to celebrate? Christmas, when they'd mapped every star in the heavens and found no God. Harvest Festival, when the crops were all dead. Valentine's Day, when it was obvious love hadn't transplanted out here any better than the seeds. Spring Equinox, on a planet that had no seasons.

She followed him outside. "It's family time," she said, resting a light hand on his shoulder.

He laughed. Family: another concept that had ceased to have any meaning a long time ago.

"Why don't you give up?" he said, without knowing what he was referring to. Give up on trying to respect traditions they had no use for? On getting anyone else to care? On trying to get anything in this godforsaken place to go right? On trying to live here at all? On her broken marriage to his bastard father? On him? On all of the above?

She didn't answer. Maybe she was having just as much trouble narrowing it down.

He shook her hand off and walked to the edge of the slope, shading his eyes from the hard southern sun. They'd built the house on high ground because his father said it would provide a spectacular view when the bioengineering was finished. By now, Halden should have been looking down on a patchwork of fields in green and yellow, bordered by fresh streams in sparking blue. Citrus orchards, polka-dotted with orange. The whole area was supposed to have been renewed, re-upholstered in different patterns and vibrant, primary colours.

But the first pass had failed, and then the second. And the third, and the fourth.

And now, all he saw was the flat, dusty red of rock, scree and sand. And in the distance, the black edge of the bloodflowers.

Yeah. Great view.

He swigged from his beer bottle. It tasted warm and gritty, but then so did most things.

"Halden," she called. A footstep crunched on the gravel, then silence.

He didn't turn round. She wouldn't dare come any closer to the edge. The sweetly seductive edge.

"Please, Hal. It's not safe."

He snorted. "So I suppose I should come back inside, right? Because it's so much safer there."

Again, she didn't respond. He was definitely coming out with the stumpers today.

He kicked at the ground, and heard her intake of breath behind him. Shards broke off and skittered down the slope. At the rate it was eroding, she wouldn't have to go anywhere near the edge. She could stay in the house and wait for it to come to her.

"You can call this the first day of spring if you like, but that isn't going to make it real," he said. His voice sounded small and tinny in his ears. "There's no such thing, not any more. Not for us. We're never going to see apple blossom again, or daffodils, or cute little lambs running around in picture-book meadows. So what's the point, Mum? What's the point in standing in the middle of all this dust and going on about life, and renewal, and the wheel of the year? What's the point of planting trees that you know are going to be dead in three months' time?"

More silence.

In the stale, motionless air, sound travelled a long way. The bloodflowers were miles off, but he could already hear snatches of their song. And their scent, of course. Rich and warm, it wasn't unpleasant at first. But the underlying notes soon came through, metallic and rotten.

His father had given them their official scientific name, but since it was in Latin and had fifteen syllables, nobody else ever used it. To the rest of the colony they were always bloodflowers, even though that was itself a misnomer: they were fauna, not flora.

Halden pinched his nostrils shut, but it was either put up with the smell or breathe though his mouth and end up with his tongue and teeth coated in dust. He clamped his lips together and squinted into the distance. The edge of the field—herd?—looked closer already. Moving fast. He imagined he could see them gently twisting in their endless fractal patterns.

"Halden. Please, come away from there."

His turn to say nothing.

He glanced back at her, bleached-out in the brightness. She lifted her hair off her neck, exposing pale track-lines of sweat in the dirt covering her skin. More lines striped her cheeks.

"It's symbolic," she said. "Observing the same rituals that people have carried out for thousands of years. It doesn't matter if the specifics don't match. We're celebrating our heritage, re-connecting with where we came from."

Halden laughed again. Or tried to—it burned his chest and he doubled over, panting. His fingers found the scar on his arm, traced the lines and marks of a hundred old cuts and bruises. A hundred attempts at defiance. A hundred lessons learned.

What an accident-prone boy, people had said. Must get it from his mother.

The bloodflowers' song swelled in his ears, resonant and harmonious.

He clenched his swollen hand, the grazed knuckles stinging as badly as the grit in his eyes. He could barely remember what had started the fight, now. Couldn't remember if he'd been pushed, insulted or ridiculed. If he'd been provoked at all. All he remembered was rage and blood.

Afterwards, he'd cried. He was supposed to be better than his father. It was the one thing he'd sworn to himself. That he'd be *better*.

"We do this because it reminds us that wherever we go, we're still human," his mother said. "We're still the same people."

Halden closed his eyes. "I don't need reminding of that," he said, and stopped resisting the call of that sharp red edge.

As he tumbled down the slope, he saw her face appear above him. Her lips were moving, but whatever she said was lost amid the ringing in his ears and the calling of the bloodflowers. He closed his eyes as the jagged rocks tore at his clothes, his skin. It sounded like they were singing his name.

Michelle Ann King *writes SF, dark fantasy and horror from her kitchen table in Essex, England. Her stories have appeared in various venues, includ-ing* Daily Science Fiction, Penumbra Magazine, *and* Drabblecast. *She loves Las Vegas, vampire films and good Scotch whisky. Find details of her stories and books at www.transientcactus.co.uk*

Playing Games with Death

John Grey

Death doesn't play chess.
Its game is dominoes.
None of that masking life's desperation
with cold wooden pieces crawling slowly,
nervously, across a board fall of threat.
The reaper much prefers
tiles lined up and squeezed together,
so that one prod from his long
snake-like fingers, and everything topples.
And death has little time to explain the rules.
It merely holds up each domino in turn,
hisses, "This is a year and this is a year
and this is a year."
No king, no checkmate.
No gradual buildup of forces
until breath and heartbeat surrender.
His hand will merely hover over your shoulder.
Then one tap and all falls down…

John Grey *is an Australian born poet, works as financial systems analyst. Recently published in* Bryant Poetry Review, Tribeca Poetry Review *and the horror anthology,* What Fears Become*with work upcoming in* Potomac Review, Hurricane Review *and* Osiris.

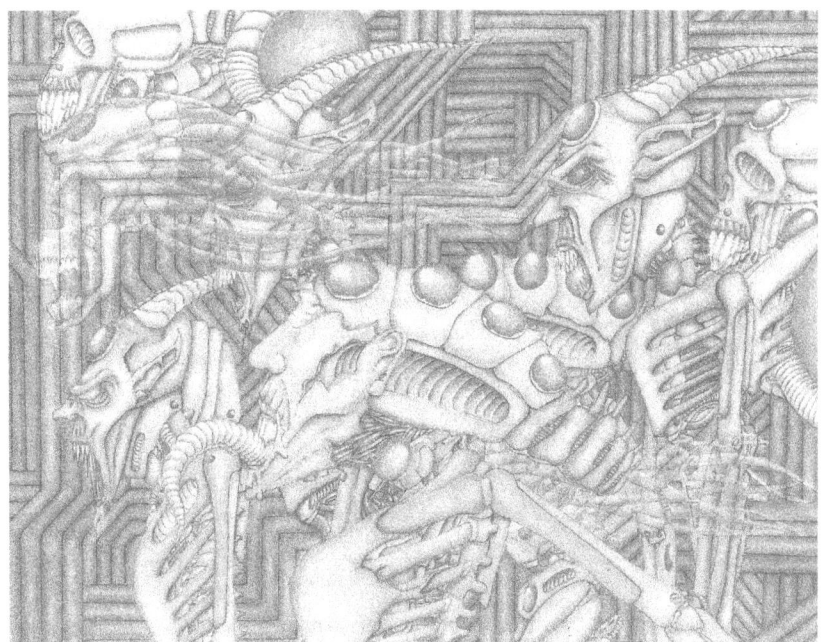

WICKED HYBRID *by R. J. Smuin*

R.J. Smuin *was born on December 7th 1978, in Burley Idaho to a family of creative eccentric minds, At a very young age he found an interest in creating art. He filled many sketchbooks with his drawings. He is mostly a self taught Artist, who created his art by experimenting with different tools to create his drawings, his favorite mediums which he often combines together being graphite, and black ink. His love for dark subject matter has always been a part of him as an inspiration. In 1997 he began a collection of art he calls the Reflection of Death collection. This collection now contains over 150 installments, and created with a technique he has revolutionized called the spiral swirl technique. He has exhibited his work in numerous gallery exhibits, and several private collectors own his work. Other endeavors he enjoys creatively are, the creation of Fantasy images, Graphic Novels, Graphic design, and Tattoo Art. His current projects include his web business, freelance designing, and an ongoing Graphic Novel series. He lives alone at his studio, in Salt Lake City, Utah.*

Interested in seeing and learning more about R.J. Smuin, go to www.sinistervisionproductions.com

The Secret of Love is Perfect Timing

H. L. Fullerton

Six hours to fly to Paradise for our honeymoon. Bevka and I had met at work: a creature feature. I played the monster's stunt double—all green screen shots so my short stature wasn't an issue; she was a runaway special effects artist. It was Los Angeles love. Both of us were the black sheep of our respective families: I was expected to become an accountant; she a mortician. Despite my difficulty walking on sand, Hawaii seemed the perfect place to celebrate. We never should've visited the volcano, at least not when it was active.

Five seconds for my skin to boil. Standing on the shore, her hand resting on my shoulder, my cheek against the curve of her hip, we watched lava bubble into the sea. Rising steam hid the wave's approach. A surfer dude ran by, pushed us toward higher ground. "Run," he yelled, but my legs weren't fast enough. I pulled my hand from Bevka's so I wouldn't slow her. The last thing I saw was Bevka— safe—before the water drove me into the sand, flayed my blistering flesh with salt and volcanic teardrops, and tried to suck me out to sea. If only I'd died then.

Four months of skin grafts. Bevka hovering in hospital corners, unable to touch me. Her eyes, wide and worried. With mine, I begged her to pull the plug. But she wouldn't. "I can fix this," she said. "I never should've let go. I won't now." She stole me from the hospital. I woke encased, trapped in a body, whether it's my ruined husk or one of her casted creations, I'm not sure. I cannot move except for my eyeballs, but my mind works and the pain is gone. I suspect Bevka's family is something more than morticians; however, they definitely work with the dead and the disfigured.

Three feet tall I stand once more. The soles of my black orthopedic shoes nailed to a red disk to keep me upright. Dressed in my wedding finery — dark gray suit with navy satin trim, pinstriped waistcoat pulled tight across my barreled chest, white shirt, burgundy ascot with pearl stickpin (my grandfather's), top hat and my pocketwatch (also Grandpa Bailey's) tucked away — I appear almost myself. But the latex mask swathing my head is transfixed and I have no voice. "I can't get the skin right. It keeps sloughing off," Bevka says, not looking at me. "I may have to call my cousin Gorrie." Gorrie comes for dinner and they fight over my presence. He says: "Puppets don't belong out. Where is his trunk?" Bevka insists, as her husband, I stand at the head of the table. They speak in their native tongue and I can't follow the conversation. Bevka bangs her hand on the table — Gorrie won't share the secret of skin with her. I'm not surprised when he waits for her to fall asleep, then carries me out to his van and lays me in an antique trunk lined with cotton batting and silk. I think, *This is what my casket would've felt like*, and close my eyes. I won't mind being buried. Not as long as I can dream of Bevka.

Two marks walk by, holding hands. The woman — her complexion ruddy — averts her eyes from my bulging ones. Her pockmarked lover snickers at Gorrie's handiwork. He's stripped me of Bevka's loving recreation of my smiling features and replaced it with a mask fit for a hellish sideshow barker. The lock of Bevka's hair that once hung over my heart droops over my latex lip in parody. Propped atop my casket-trunk, I have never been so tall. I stare into the crowd, searching for Bevka's face in every passerby. Does she mourn me? Is she looking for me? If she rescues me this one more time, I'll tell her our parting was necessary. Yes, I'm an object of ridicule in Gorrie's traveling puppet show, but none of that matters because I've guessed the secret of skin. Like love, it has to be real to last.

One chance is all I'll get. I've loosened the nails in my shoes with persistent rocking. The longer I'm in my body — and it is mine, I can tell now, Bevka didn't empty me the way Gorrie empties his creations into blocks of wood or stuffed cloth — the more control I can exert over it. Not much, but enough to topple myself from my coffin. Enough to grab some poor stranger should they stray near. My arms spread as if I'm about to hug the world, it should be easy to wrap my hands around a curious body and sink my teeth into soft neck, wrap myself in its perfect flesh and return home to my bride. In this dusky light, it is difficult to pick out my victim — I want to look good for Bevka — but

I may have to settle for any soul brave enough to duck under the rope barricade Gorrie has strung around my display. From the corner of my eye, I spot a group of drunk frat boys elbowing each other. Approaching on a dare. I wriggle my feet and sway atop my box. A boy comes so close the spotlights brush his skin—illuminating flesh, so clear, so smooth, so unscarred. Taller than me, he has plenty of skin to go around. Closer, I urge, closer. He takes another step, laughs over his shoulder at his friends.

Now. I leap. My heart sings. Bevka, honey, I'm coming.

H.L. Fullerton *(whose short fiction can be found in* Dagan Books, Andromeda Spaceways Inflight Magazine, Bards and Sages, *and* Penumbra) *thinks short stories are more interesting than biographies.*

Writing as a Near-Death Experience

J. J. Steinfeld

I start to count every story
I had ever written
at first slowly
then picking up speed
like a frightened runner
running from a newly discovered
venomous creature with fragrant poison
for which there is no known antidote
then before reaching
my most recent story
I begin to count the words
in every story I had ever written
counting by tens and twenties
and settling in to blocks
of a hundred words
forgetting about anything
that might be pursuing me
reaching an incomplete total
that looked like a faraway something
I didn't have a name for
then I decided to quit all the counting
and start a new story
about a venomous creature
that catches a writer and
is just about to demonstrate
its reason for being.

Canadian poet, fiction writer, and playwright J. J. Steinfeld *lives on Prince Edward Island, where he is patiently waiting for Godot's arrival and a phone call from Kafka. While waiting, he has published fourteen books, including* **Should the Word Hell Be Capitalized?** *(Stories, Gaspereau Press),* **Would You Hide Me?** *(Stories, Gaspereau Press),* **An Affection for Precipices** *(Poetry, Serengeti Press),* **Misshapenness** *(Poetry, Ekstasis Editions),* **Word Burials** *(Novel and Stories, Crossing Chaos Enigmatic Ink), and* **A Glass Shard and Memory** *(Stories, Recliner Books). More than three hundred of his short stories and nearly six hundred poems have appeared in anthologies and periodicals internationally, and over forty of his one-act plays and a handful of full-length plays have been performed in Canada and the United States.*

My Big Problem with Zombies

Phil Beloin, Jr.

Sure, I'm a sarcastic mutherfucker. But that's how I deal. Many soldiers do this. The bastards have breached the Farmington River, dozens of'em, and they're stagger-stepping my way.

1) How do they get out of the grave when they can hardly punch thru the particleboard over a window?

2) Stumbling around like drunks on a three-day bender, why don't they try and get into a car to drive home? That's what I used to do.

3) After grandma — or any loved one for that matter — dies of natural causes, put a bullet in their fucking brain or, shit, anyone know how to build a guillotine? Slice/chop/plop. This would prevent future zombie infestations.

4) Sex with a zombie? Definitely a possibility, though you'll need rope, tape, or, if possible, dental forceps… Are zombies even capable of love, or at the very least, some kind of feelings?

5) They swim like Michael Phelps after several humongous bong hits. Why don't they sink, get swept away in the current, snagged on a downed tree, or somethin'?

Not much time left now. I got one bullet left. A hollow point. And you know where I'm putting it.

Editor's note: This unsigned writing was discovered on a body near the Heublein Tower atop Avon Mountain. This blog remains dedicated to identifying all of our Connecticut war dead. Queries as to the identity of this hero can be emailed to:

EDITOR@KIA.MIA.CTZOMBIEWAR.blogspot.com

Phil Beloin Jr. *is the author of the crime novel,* The Big Bad. **Full Dark City Press** *will be publishing his novella,* Revenge Is A Redhead, *next year. Phil lives in Connecticut near the Heublein Tower.*

Subscribe to

BÊTE NOIRE

1 year, 4 issues
$23.95*

Send email to: subscribe @betenoiremagazine.com

Or fill out the form below and send, along with check or
money order made payable to Jennifer Gifford to:

P.O. Box 1545
Highland, MI 48357

Name:_____

Address: _____

Email:_____

Susbcription includes Dark Opus Press's annual anthnology

*US and Canada only, international subscriptions $29.95/year